THREE MEN
WENT TO WAR

Three Men Went to War

DAVID NEWMAN

Based on an original screenplay by
TREVOR PEACOCK

NEW ENGLISH LIBRARY
TIMES MIRROR

A New English Library Original Publication 1978
© 1978 by David Newman

*

FIRST NEL PAPERBACK EDITION APRIL 1978

*

NEL Books are published by
New English Library Limited from Barnard's Inn, Holborn, London EC1N 2JR
Made and printed in Great Britain by Hunt Barnard Printing Ltd., Aylesbury, Bucks.

45003641 3

Chapter 1

In 1915 the Turkish Empire stretched from the Mediterranean to the Persian Gulf, a vast expanse of fertile land, deserts, mountains, rivers, cities, villages and subject peoples. It was ramshackle, badly governed and poor. Little had changed in centuries, but change was on the way.

Early in the Great War the Germans took care to get the Turkish rulers on their side. Not for the sake of the men that could be conscripted into armies, but for a reason even the Turks themselves did not suspect: beneath the sands of its eastern regions lay hidden a priceless possession – oil. The Turks were hardly aware of it, and certainly had no conception of its worth.

The German High Command had. They saw that oil was the key to twentieth-century military power and industrial expansion. Oil could power the factories that made rifles and cannon. Oil could keep their armies mobile in the field when they eventually broke through the trench lines and drove the British and French back to the Channel. Oil could power the newfangled aeroplanes that might one day be a new navy of the skies.

German military and engineering experts were sent to Turkey, to survey, to plan, to advise and to mobilise the shambling Turkish war effort into something that would be of use to German plans.

Late as ever, Whitehall saw the threat. Germans were moving into Mesopotamia alongside the Turks; something had to be done quickly. A British strike force was sent from the handiest place – India. And so the orders were given, the troop-ships sailed and on the day that Turkey officially declared war on the Allies, the British expeditionary force from India steamed into the Persian Gulf, horse, foot and guns.

Mesopotamia had been the birthplace of European civilisation. But that was before the Arabs and the Turks came. To the British troops marching inland, it was a hot and dusty place, with not a decent drink to be had and not much in the way of women either. They slogged up the course of the Tigris river until they made contact with the oncoming Turkish army, and the fighting began.

At first it was disorganised and easy, mostly skirmishing, where the British and Indian riflemen outclassed the Turks and pushed them back. But as the Turks fell back and the British pushed on after them, supply lines back to base were getting longer and longer and had to be protected all the time. General Townshend began to have serious doubts about the campaign he had been ordered to mount: just how far could he push the Turks, stretching his own forces thinner and thinner? Reinforcements and supplies from India were slow to arrive and there was no obvious reason why the Turks should give up, however far they were forced back.

Whitehall had made a major mistake, one of many that was costly in other men's lives. Three hundred miles north of their base, and almost in sight of Baghdad, the British discovered that the Turks were not so stupid as they seemed at first sight. Their long retreat had drawn the British army into a trap.

South of Baghdad the Turks made a determined stand. And by now they outnumbered and outgunned the British. Two days of fighting showed General Townshend that his advance was at an end and that he would never take the city with the force at his disposal. He was losing men fast and running low on ammunition and food. There was nothing to do but pull back to a position he could hold until reinforcements arrived.

The British extricated themselves from the fighting and fell back, harassed all the way, to the town of Kut, a hundred miles south of Baghdad. The Tigris was in its annual flood and Kut was surrounded by swamps. The British dug in round the town and waited for relief, while the Turks moved up and surrounded them. The long siege of Kut had begun and fifty thousand British troops were pinned down and unable to break out.

Further south, the forces left in base camps and staging posts could do little but fly sorties against the Turks and their installations with the few planes they had.

At a Royal Flying Corps airfield, Lieutenant Francis Holt was studying a batch of aerial photographs on a trestle table in the tent alongside a makeshift landing strip. Holt had been in the RFC three months and took his job seriously.

The Flying Corps was in its infancy. Even though Holt was an American he had had no difficulty in joining up as a volunteer, particularly as he had attended Military Academy and had intended to join the United States army. But America was not in the European war as yet and Holt did not want to wait. Aeroplanes attracted him. He sailed for England and joined up. His training as an air-gunner and bomber had lasted exactly six weeks before he found himself on the way to Mesopotamia to be attached to the British army there.

Captain White came into the tent. He was Holt's pilot, a big exuberant schoolboy of a man who loved flying and fighting. Like Holt, he was twenty-one years old.

'Come on, time to go,' he said cheerfully.

Holt tapped the pictures with his finger.

'Seeing that you're flying the crate, don't you think you should take a look at these photos? They give a view of the whole route.'

White waved them away with a grin.

'Don't worry – you won't get lost with me. I could find my way there and back blindfold.'

'It's a great set of pictures.'

White chuckled.

'I've got a better set of pictures in my tent I bought off a native in Port Said. You wouldn't believe what the bints get up to. Make your hair curl!'

They were about to leave when the Commanding Officer came into the tent. He glanced at the photos while the two young men waited.

'Good enough,' he said. 'You've handled explosives before, Holt?'

'Yes, sir.'

'Good – it calls for more skill than heaving bombs over the side on to enemy installations and troops. Now, on this mission bear in mind that it's not enough just to bring the telegraph wires down. You must destroy the insulators as well. I'm quite sure the Turks are capable of putting new telegraph posts up, but I doubt if they have the training to connect the wires properly if the insulators have to be replaced.'

'You don't want us to put down at Kut this morning, sir?' Holt asked.

'No, we've nothing for them today. The important job is to cut Johnny Turk's communications into Baghdad and out of Baghdad to the force hemming our chaps in at Kut. You've been briefed already – your first landing is on the flat ground near Yusufiya.'

Outside the tent an engine coughed and started up.

'Off you go. Good luck.'

Holt and White went out to where a mechanic was warming up the engine of their plane. Holt climbed into the rear seat and an armourer handed him up a wooden box of explosives and detonators. He stowed it carefully under his seat.

Meanwhile White was talking to the mechanic, Roberts, who was carrying out his pre-flight check.

'Juice?'

'Twenty gallons, sir.'

'Oil?'

'Topped up to a gallon and a half. All braces, flying wires, wheels and canvas checked and correct, sir.'

'She'll do. Got the eggs?'

8

The mechanic climbed out of the cockpit and White got in. Roberts had a box on the ground and from it he took a tall glass, two eggs and a bottle of Worcester sauce. He handed the ingredients up to White, who broke the eggs into the glass, tipped a liberal measure of Worcester sauce in and swallowed the lot in one gulp.

'Right, you little Turkish delights – we're coming to get you!' White sang out. 'Chocks away!'

He gunned the engine as the men on the ground pulled away the chocks from under the wheels. The men took a wing-tip each as the plane wobbled forward and turned on to the strip. White gave them a thumbs-up and they stood clear as he opened up the throttle and rolled down the strip, gathering speed. In the rear seat Holt strapped in and relaxed as he felt the tail come up off the ground. He had every confidence in his Australian pilot.

The slip-stream was rushing into his face and past the big goggles that protected his eyes. He heard White carol 'Wahoo!' as he eased the stick back and the plane lifted off the bumpy ground and started its climb.

They flew north for an hour, with Holt scanning the ground below all the way and comparing it with the map he held on his knees. It was almost featureless: brown, scrubby low hills here and there. Nearly desert. Now and again a small village. A poor place to crash-land and an even poorer place to have to live in, Holt reflected.

Over to the left he saw a faint dust-cloud. He stared at it for a while through his binoculars until he had it clear. It was a column of men, pack animals and some cavalry. They had to be Turks on their way to Kut with supplies for the besieging force.

He tapped White on the shoulder and pointed down. White stared until he found the point of interest and then reacted joyously by putting the plane into a dive and banking towards the column.

The moment he was in range, White opened up with the machine-gun mounted on the fuselage in front of him. It was synchronised with the propeller to fire through it without hitting the blades. All the pilot had to do was keep the plane pointing at the target and press the firing-button.

The column scattered as the plane came roaring down at it and the machine-gun bullets stitched a line of dust-puffs across the ground and through the scattering column itself. Craning over the side as the plane zoomed over them to bank and come in again, Holt saw one or two horses and men kicking on the ground.

White banked fast and came in to zap the column again. By now the men and animals were bolting in all directions. He chased a little group and gunned them down, came round for a third pass and sprayed everything that still moved. The men were lying flat, pressed to the ground, but he got a horse or two, which was as good, since it would make it all the harder for the survivors to get their supplies to the front.

Singing horribly out of tune, White climbed the plane again and went back on to his original course. The job they had been given to do was a boring one – shooting up the Turkish column had been a welcome diversion.

In another twenty minutes they picked out the line of telegraph posts they were after. The posts marched in a straight line across the blank landscape, until they vanished from sight in both directions. White pointed down and put the plane into a long sweeping curve that would land it alongside the wires.

On the descent Holt ducked down into the cockpit and opened up his box of bangs. He wanted to have them sorted out and ready so that he could plant the demolition charges, get the job done and be back up in the sky as soon as possible. He hadn't spotted any movement on the ground, but you could never be sure in this sort of country. There could be a Turkish patrol or even half a battalion hidden behind the next flat hill, waiting to open up when the plane put down.

White put the plane into a long slow glide. As the wheels touched down, a gust of wind took the tail. The plane swerved sideways and bumped up into the air again. Unready for it, Holt was thrown forward in the cockpit and banged his head on the fuselage. Shaking his head to clear it, he could hear

White swearing at the top of his voice as he struggled to regain control.

Still moving fast, the plane was heading straight for a telegraph post. White fought it, spun it round and was almost clear. But not quite – there was a splitting crunch as his starboard wing hit the pole, then the tail swung round again and the plane stopped at last.

'God damn and blast this bloody junk-heap of a flaming kite,' White bawled, his face red with anger.

Holt rubbed his forehead.

'That was a bit careless,' he said.

'Don't blame me – the bloody wind caught the tail as the wheels touched and tore the stick out of my hand.'

He switched the engine off. Holt stood up in the cockpit and looked carefully all around. The landscape seemed empty enough.

'I thought you said we wouldn't get lost,' Holt reminded White.

'We're not lost, sport. We're just stuck in the mud. Different bloody thing.'

He took a long look round the horizon himself and grunted. Holt looked in the direction he pointed and saw, very far away, coming over a low ridge, a column of cavalry.

'Let's hope they don't realise we're stuck,' said Holt. 'They might get nasty. You get on with the running repairs while I do my little blow-up job.'

He got out of the plane and trotted over to the next telegraph post with his box of explosives. Quickly, but taking care over what he was doing, he laid a necklace of gun-cotton round the base of the pole and then, very delicately, fixed in a detonator. He had intended to demolish six poles in a row, but with trouble on the way, one would have to do for now. At least it would cut the line until the Turks got someone out to this godforsaken spot with the skill to repair it.

He glanced over his shoulder. The horsemen were very much closer. They were coming on at a canter, not a gallop, as if uncertain about the situation. Maybe they've never seen a plane before, Holt thought. Or they don't know what kind of armament we've got.

He inserted a mercury fulminate pencil with a fuse attached into the detonator. The drumming of horses' hooves was suddenly very loud in his ears. He looked up from what he was doing. The horsemen had understood at last what he was about with the telegraph post and were coming at a gallop to stop him.

They were about two hundred yards away as Holt lit the fuse and ran like hell for the plane, lugging his box.

The charges went up when the horsemen were fifty yards from the post. Horses reared and shied and threw their riders, while the men at the rear shouted and galloped on as the post toppled over and brought the wires down with it.

White had completed his inspection of the plane. The leading edge of the lower starboard wing was smashed and a strut between the two wings was broken through. One of the wheels was bent on the landing gear. He was doing what he could to patch up the wing when Holt reached the plane, scrambled into the cockpit and emerged with a big spanner. To White's amazement, he ran back to the fallen telegraph post and began to smash the insulators with the spanner.

The Turks had fallen back some way, but they were off their horses and had unslung their rifles. They opened fire on Holt.

'Hey, Francis!' White shouted. 'Those bastards mean business. Let's get going.'

He climbed into the cockpit while Holt ran back, bullets kicking up dust about him.

'Swing the prop!' White yelled. 'For Christ's sake hurry up!'

Holt threw away the spanner and spun the prop with both hands. The enemy were running towards the plane now, firing as they came.

'Again!'

Holt spun it again and the engine started with a roar and a belch of smoke. He scrambled aboard as White opened up the throttle and the plane went lurching over the bumpy ground.

White steered straight towards the shouting and firing Turks. They fled before him and he gunned his engine to get lift-off speed. The plane hopped once or twice but it stayed on the ground, creaking and rattling at the beating it was taking.

By now the enemy had mounted up and were galloping after them. Some of them were waving long swords and some were firing their rifles.

'Come up, you bastard!' White roared at the plane as he hauled the stick back.

The machine lifted off the ground, its engine screaming. It climbed six feet and then dropped like a stone, the controls dead. It went racing and leaping over the sand and rocks, swaying and bouncing, until the wheels hit a big rock. The tail went up in the air, the nose went down and the plane jarred to a bone-breaking stop, a complete wreck.

White and Holt hung dazed and breathless in their straps.

The enemy force rode up and surrounded them. There was a Turkish officer, three Turkish soldiers and about twenty dirty-looking Arabs on skinny horses. The officer spurred his frightened horse up close to the plane and held out his hand to Holt. Holt unfastened his seat belt and took the offered hand as he climbed down to the ground.

The officer smiled at him in a friendly fashion. Holt took that as a good sign and was about to recite his name, rank and number, as the book said, when he was grabbed from behind and pulled to the ground.

Half a dozen Arabs piled on to him. Holt kicked and fought, thinking they meant to kill him with their bare hands, but there were too many of them. They ripped off his flying helmet and jacket and stripped him down to his vest and underpants. Then they let go. Holt sat up, shaken and surprised, to see White on the ground under a scrum of Arabs, his clothes also being torn off. After a while, the Turkish officer spoke to his three men, who drove the Arabs off White with their riding whips.

White sat up, shaking his head. He and Holt looked in amazement at the Turkish officer and then at the Arabs donning odd items of Royal Flying Corps clothing. The officer smiled and spread his hands out as if to say 'Arabs will be Arabs.'

The three Turkish soldiers led White and Holt away from the plane to where they had a spare horse waiting. Holt looked back over his shoulder and saw the Arabs swarming over the wrecked plane, ripping out the seats, instruments and anything else that would come lose. One of them found the machine-gun button by accident and fired a burst down into the ground. They tried to get the gun off its mounts, but failing, fired at point-blank range at the mounts with their rifles to break them.

'For God's sake!' Holt said to the nearest soldier. 'That plane's loaded with explosives – if they hit the petrol tank, the lot will go sky-high. You've got to stop them!'

But they did not understand what he meant and urged him towards the waiting horse. Behind him was the sound of the petrol tank exploding and almost immediately afterwards an even louder explosion that blew the plane apart. Holt and White flung themselves to the ground as sand and fragments of the plane rained down.

When the dust and smoke settled, Holt got up and looked at the wreck again. Several of the Arabs had been killed outright and many were burned and injured badly. The others ignored the dead and wounded and the bits of bodies scattered around and got on with their looting. They even took the dead men's clothes and equipment.

'What kind of people are they?' Holt asked in astonishment.

The Turkish officer shrugged and smiled his 'Arabs will be Arabs' smile again.

His men tied White's and Holt's hands behind their backs and put them on the same horse. It was only then that Holt fully realised that he was a prisoner of war, among people he knew nothing about and whose language and customs were incomprehensible to him.

Chapter 2

At the end of what seemed an endless ride in the searing heat, they came to the village of Yusufiya. At least, that's what it sounded like to Holt when the Turkish officer pointed to it and told him its name.

It looked as if it had grown out of the earth. Three or four short streets of tiny mud and timber houses, dusty, sun-baked and crumbling. But at least people live here, Holt told himself. It had to be better than being out in the wilderness.

But it wasn't.

As the little procession of Turks and Arabs rode in with their prisoners, the whole population of Yusufiya turned out to enjoy the spectacle. Thin ragged men and children danced and shouted along both sides of the horses. For one second Holt thought it was a welcome parade. But then he saw that the Arabs were threatening and cursing – their intent was plain enough even though the shouted abuse meant nothing to the prisoners.

Veiled women in tatty black robes stayed in the shelter of doorways, but they too were shaking their fists and screaming insults. One or two of them pulled down their veils to reveal prematurely old faces while they drew fingers across their throats to show the prisoners what was in store for them. An old man wearing only a grubby loin-cloth ran beside the horses brandishing an ancient sword.

'Don't think much of the welcome,' said White, trying to stay cheerful.

It got worse. The crowd pushed the soldiers aside and pulled the two bound men from the horse and knocked them about, punching, kicking, even swinging and poking at them with heavy sticks. The Turks dismounted and hustled the prisoners along, whipping the crowd back as best they could.

At the end of the street stood the village lock-up – a squat and ramshackle building of baked mud with a solid wooden door. It was only a short street but Holt and White were badly beaten and bleeding before they got to the jail and were roughly pushed inside.

Even then they were not safe. The crowd outside jostled for a place at the one small grilled window, to shout and spit and throw stones at them.

Bruised and battered, the two men stood swaying in the small dark cell that formed the whole jail. It was empty except for a bad smell. White looked very groggy. Holt, blood trickling down his cheek from a cut over the eye, pulled him over to the wall where the window was and made him sit down with his back to it. This was the only safe place from the stones being thrown at them.

Holt eased himself down beside the pilot, wincing at the contusions he had acquired in the last five minutes.

'Friendly bastards,' he said. 'I guess they don't like foreigners round here.'

White was silent. His cheerfulness had run out.

'Hell, my war didn't last long,' Holt went on, trying to keep White from getting too demoralised. 'Still, I don't think we'll be stuck too long in this hell-hole. There's a British force south of here. They'll come looking for us when we don't report back to base. And Kut's not all that far. There'll be a column on the way soon to help the big break-out.'

He looked at White and noticed that his face was very pale and his eyes were staring.

'You OK?' he asked.

When White still said nothing, Holt touched him. The front of his vest was sticky with blood. Anxiously he pulled up the vest and in the gloom of the cell he saw the knife wound between the Australian's ribs.

'Some bastard got you in the crowd,' he said softly.

White rallied for a moment.

'Don't think I can wait for that big break-out, sport,' he whispered.

He coughed and blood oozed from his mouth. Holt stared in fear as White's eyes closed slowly.

'My God – he's dying!' he exclaimed.

He rushed to the cell door and banged on it and shouted for help. The faces blocking the window behind him shouted and spat.

Holt turned to them and pointed to White slumped on the floor.

'He's dying!' he shouted to the uncomprehending jeerers. 'Get help before he bleeds to death.'

The onlookers fell silent, puzzled by his vehemence. Then one of them hoisted up his rags and pissed in through the window. The others laughed and soon they were all at it.

Holt hauled White away from the splashing and stinking streams to a corner. He felt for a pulse and couldn't find it. He put his hand on White's bloody chest and there was no heart-beat.

White was dead and Holt was really frightened for the first time in his life.

At nightfall the crowd dispersed. Worn out by the beating and shock, Holt dozed fitfully on the trodden earth floor, thirsty and hungry. White's body was cold and too stiff to be moved.

It was nearly noon before the door was opened and one of the Turkish soldiers came in with a clay pot of water and two chunks of stale black bread.

Holt showed him that White was dead and he called two Arabs in to haul the body away. He left the food and water and locked the door behind him. Holt was alone. And he stayed alone in the cell for the next four weeks, never let outside and always half-starved. For the first day or two the villagers tormented him from the window, then they got bored and left him. Except for the children. They never seemed to tire of baiting him and he never knew when a

2

sharp-edged rock would come flying through the grille. He was tempted to throw them back but decided that if he hit anyone it would enrage their parents and make things worse for him.

He kept count of the days by scratching the mud wall with a pointed stone. On the twenty-ninth day, when two Turkish soldiers came and led him out of the stink of his own excrement, his eyes had become so used to the semi-darkness that the daylight blinded him for a while.

They hoisted him up on to a horse and trotted out of the village, one on either side of him. It was useless to try to talk to them. They had no language in common, and even if they had, the Turks would probably not have answered him. They seemed to take a very tough line with prisoners.

It was three days ride to Samarra. After the ugliness of the village where he had been held for so long, Holt was staggered by the beauty of the city. Buildings of white sand-stone reflected the sunlight. Tall minarets had necklaces of golden mosaic round them. The gilded domes of the mosques stood out against the emerald green of grass and palm-leaves. Holt almost wept with relief when he saw these signs of civilisation ahead of him.

The escort guided him into the city and down narrow cobbled streets. They had taken pity on his near nakedness and given him a torn and dirty Turkish army shirt and a pair of trousers to put on. He felt scruffy and humiliated, but his hope was growing that in this city his ordeal among the savages would be over. He scratched the month's growth of beard on his chin and thought longingly about a shave and a bath.

In Samarra the people paid very little attention to the three men riding through the streets. And that is a good sign, Holt told himself – at least they don't beat up prisoners on sight.

The escort halted him by a doorway with an armed sentry. Holt dismounted and while one of the Turks looked after the horses, the other took him inside. He found himself in the office of the Turkish commandant.

18

The room was far from impressive. The walls were scarred and dirty, the floor unswept. But the commandant sat behind a desk with a marble top.

Holt's escort handed over his papers and was waved away. He left without a word, presumably to ride back with his companion to the village. Holt stood silent while the Turkish officer studied his papers. He wondered what the man would make of them.

The officer looked at him.

'I am Ghani Bey,' he said in accented but understandable English. 'I am commandant here in Samarra. Your name is Lieutenant Holt and you fly aeroplanes, yes?'

'I did.'

'In the air?'

'Sure. We tried it in the sand and it didn't work out.'

Ghani Bey did not understand the joke.

'Excuse me, please?' he said, scowling.

'I fly aeroplanes, in the air, yes,' said Holt, not wanting to antagonise him.

Ghani Bey got up and came round the desk to face Holt from about three feet away. His hand rested on the pistol in his belt.

'Do you drop bombs on holy mosques?'

There was menace in his voice.

'No, never,' said Holt shortly.

'You were captured on the twenty-fifth of April it says in your papers?'

'That's right. And since that time I've been kept in a filthy cage and starved to death. But there's something more important than that. I wish to make an official protest about the murder of my pilot after we were taken prisoner and were unarmed and not attempting to escape.'

The Turk drew his pistol slowly and checked it.

'Yes?' he said.

'It was contrary to all conventions of war,' Holt persisted stubbornly.

Ghani Bey pointed the pistol to the left of Holt and fired

19

it at the wall. The report seemed very loud in the small office. Holt stood still.

'German-made,' said the Turk approvingly. 'We have many fine guns now that the Germans are our allies.'

'Let's hope you don't learn how to use them,' said Holt, angry at the way his protest was being shrugged off.

The Turk thought it over and then pointed his pistol at Holt's belly.

'If I shoot you, no one will ask why. I am commandant here. You understand?'

Before Holt could react to that, four soldiers came into the room carrying cooking pots. Maybe they were taking a short cut to the mess hall, Holt thought. That would be about right for the standard of discipline he had seen – short cut through the commanding officer's office.

Ghani Bey shouted at the men, smacked one of them across the face, and sent them packing. Then, his anger exhausted, he sat at his desk again and put his pistol away.

'Do you know that we have won the war against you, Lieutenant Holt?' he asked with a sunny smile. 'Kut has surrendered.'

Holt was stunned.

'Four hundred officers and fourteen thousand men, all prisoners. Shake hands, Lieutenant Holt.'

He stretched his arm across the desk and Holt shook hands, wondering why.

'We respect British officers,' said Ghani Bey. 'You are our prisoners, but you see that we are civilised and we have a very nice respect. Your troubles are now over. All British officers will be treated as honoured guests of the Sultan. Very nice.'

He held out his hand and Holt shook it again.

Ghani Bey shouted an order and a soldier came in to lead Holt away. He took him to a large house further down the same street. There was a large wooden gate opening from the street, with a sentry on duty, and inside a courtyard with doors leading off it. At the far end a stairway led up to a balcony running round the whole courtyard, with doors opening off that too.

'I say, are you one of us?' an English voice called down from the balcony.

Holt looked up to see a youngish man in British army uniform leaning over the railing.

'I hope so,' Holt answered.

'I mean, you are British, aren't you?'

'Lieutenant Holt, Royal Flying Corps. I'm American.'

The idea seemed to amuse the other man.

'An American flyer? How did you get caught – fall out of your plane? Fancy a cup of tea, old boy? Come on up.'

Holt turned to see if this was all right with his escort, but the man had already gone.

Holt shrugged and went up the stairs to join the officer on the balcony.

'I'm Lieutenant Partridge. My friends call me Birdie. Come and meet the others.'

He led Holt through a door into a room where five men were sitting on cane chairs and chatting. In one corner was a metal bath full of water with bottles of beer bobbing about to cool.

Birdie introduced the newcomer to the senior officer.

'Sir, this is Lieutenant Holt.'

All the men in the room stared at him. He was quite a sight in his tattered Turkish shirt and trousers, with a month's beard on his face.

'Not one of us, I'm afraid, sir,' Birdie prattled on. 'He's Royal Flying Corps.'

Colonel Cottram stood up to shake hands.

'Nice to see you, Holt. Where's your home?'

'In the States, sir. New England, not far from Boston.'

'Really? I knew a fellow name of Holt. Played cricket for Essex. Any relation?'

'I don't think so, sir.'

The conversation struck Holt as utterly absurd, considering their circumstances and his own appearance.

'How did they bag you, Holt?' asked one of the others.

'We were trying to cut their communications. The pilot landed us badly and we couldn't get off the ground again. It was bad luck, I guess.'

There was a chaplain with a major's crown on his epaulettes.

'Were you one of the chaps who flew over Kut to drop bags of rice to us?' he asked.

'Not me, sir. They had me on other duties. I guess the rice was only a drop in the ocean for you.'

Birdie started to brew up over a small portable stove.

'Sit down, Holt,' said the colonel.

Holt sat. From a cage to a British tea party was slightly too much to take.

'I've only just heard about the surrender,' he said. 'They kept me locked up in some stinking village for a month. And murdered my pilot. I've complained to the commandant here but he didn't take much notice. Maybe you can do something official about it, sir. They shouldn't get away with a thing like that.'

The colonel's thoughts were elsewhere.

'We held out as long as we could,' he said. 'It was shortage of food that did for us. We ate all our gun-horses, you know.'

'And the mules,' said the captain. 'Even the donkeys. Ever eaten a donkey, Holt?'

'The mess sergeant worked wonders,' said the chaplain. 'He thought up splendid names for what he served up. Derby Day soup. And Grand National pâté – remember that one?'

Holt looked round the faces, weighing them up. They seemed to him punch-drunk. The shock of defeat by an enemy they had despised, he surmised. They were not functioning any more.

'Did you march all the way here from Kut or come on horseback?' he asked.

'Good Lord, no!' the colonel answered. 'We came by military transport. The men have to march, of course. They've been treated shabbily by the Turks. At the right time I shall put in a strong complaint, you may be sure of that.'

'What will the Turks do with them? According to Ghani

Bey there were fourteen thousand men at Kut.'

The colonel's eyes closed wearily. It was the captain who answered.

'There's a hell of a lot less now,' he said brusquely. 'We saw some pretty gruesome sights on the way here from Baghdad. You've been in the cage yourself, so you can guess what sort of treatment the men got from the natives. It sickens me to think of it. Whole companies of unarmed men beaten and massacred by natives with swords and sticks. The plain truth is, Holt, we don't know how many are still alive or what will happen to them.'

'You must remember,' said the colonel. 'This whole area of Mesopotamia is in a state of chaos and collapse. The Turks have only a weak grip on it. The natives are very primitive people to start with ... '

His train of thought seemed to wander. Suddenly he said, 'Have I introduced you to everybody? You've met Birdie Partridge. I'm Colonel Cottram, senior British officer in Samarra. This is Jack Vallance, Captain Hyde-Dunning. And our chaplain, Major Harris. And Major Pett, my adjutant.'

Birdie saw the look on Holt's face and hurried to change the conversation.

'I say – the water's boiling. Would you like a shave, old chap?'

Chapter 3

On the long march north from Kut across the sun-baked landscape, disheartened and under-fed British prisoners died slowly and painfully. The separate columns, kept small for security reasons, straggled across sand and stones, from village to village, remnants of a broken army.

The men were burnt dark brown by the unrelenting sun. Their beards grew long and unkempt, their clothes disintegrated to rags. After the first week it was almost impossible to distinguish the English prisoners from their Indian comrades.

Many of them were barefoot, eager Arabs having stolen their boots. Some had the remains of boots strapped round blistered and bleeding feet.

At the head of one particular column a Turkish sergeant rode on an ill-fed horse. He made no effort to ride fast or slow – just a steady plod that kept the prisoners moving northwards. If they died, they died. It meant nothing to Raghib Chaoush.

His orders were to take his prisoners north, from ration depot to ration depot, though there was precious little for them to eat at each one and no kind of medical attention.

Nobody had bothered to count the number of men he started with. Nobody would bother to count the number he arrived with. Whether they lived or died was their own concern, not his.

And die they did, a few each day, worn out by the endless

trudging under the sun, from malnutrition and disease, brutalised and hardly wanting to prolong the pointless agony of living.

Raghib's guards were not Turks but Askars, nomads mounted on army mules, rifles slung over their shoulders and long whips in their hands. They rode at the sides of the column and at the rear, and when anyone looked like dropping in his tracks, they lashed out with their whips.

The Askars shouted incessantly the word that would for the rest of their lives haunt those who survived the cruelties of the Kut Column – *'Yellah! Yellah!'*

The prisoners had found out on the first day of the march what it meant – 'Keep moving!' and it was invariably accompanied by a lash of the whip across the back of the nearest man, or a vicious kick.

When a man could go no further, he fell. The nearest Askar would leap from his mule and stand over him, whipping his bare shoulders and back. Sometimes the pain would force the man to his feet, to stagger along with the column again. Sometimes the man was too far gone and would lie limp and unmoving under the flogging. The Askar would kick him a few times, and if he did not respond, would remount and leave him.

The column would pass on. The man left behind would soon succumb to the sun, or thirst, or the knives of the first natives who found him.

From Kut onwards the column had left a trail of dead men half-way across the country. The natives stripped them of whatever they had and left them naked. The desert animals found them after dark and fed on them. A trail of rotting flesh and sun-bleached bones marked the way the prisoners had passed.

When the city of Samarra appeared on the distant horizon, most of them thought it was just a mirage. But it grew taller and more solid as they staggered on. They saw the domes and minarets, the white buildings. And fresh heart came into them. Whatever it was, it would be a place to rest. They moved towards it, lips cracked and parched, unable to believe

25

their luck. But they were to be disappointed.

While the other ranks suffered and died, Holt had discovered some surprising things in Samarra. The British officers lived in the big house assigned to them. There was a sentry on the gate, but that meant nothing. If they wanted to go into the town, they only had to ask the sentry to accompany them. And he went willingly as long as they gave him money.

And money they had. Birdie explained it to Holt.

'Well, you see, Johnny Turk is very keen to convince the world that he's as civilised as the rest of us. So he treats officer prisoners with respect. Mind you, we haven't got a lavatory in our quarters, but neither has the commandant. He sees we get our pay regularly. Of course, it's all pretty crooked, as you'd expect from this lot. We sign for the money they give us and then they change the figures and get twice the amount back from the War Office through a bank in a neutral country. Cosy little arrangement – we're being cheated and the War Office is being cheated. We buy all our own food and anything else we need. The Turks provide us with nothing, except the billet.'

Holt shook his head in surprise.

'Damned funny arrangement for prisoners of war, if you ask me,' he said. 'Still, I guess it's all different in this kind of place. How do you get on with the Turkish guards?'

'They're not Turks, old boy. The Turkish soldiers are all up at the front, wherever that may be now. The guards are Kurds or Arabs, only the officers are Turks. We get on all right with them because we pay their wages, but they treat other ranks like cattle.'

'How come we pay their wages? I don't get it.'

'Indirectly. The Turks don't pay them anything at all, you see, only give them a rifle and a uniform and a daily ration you wouldn't feed to the pigs at home. No money. So the guards take a little cash from us for the privilege of being escorted to the bazaar to buy food and things. And that's the only wages they get.'

'I begin to see why they're so quick off the mark when

26

there's any loot to be had. God, what a way to run an army!'

A bellowing, untuneful voice interrupted from the balcony outside:

'Life's a pudding full of plums.

Let us take it as it comes . . . '

'What in hell is that?' Holt asked.

'Gilbert and Sullivan, old boy. You wouldn't know, being a Yank.'

Holt stuck his head out of the window. On the balcony was a big man with a hawk's nose and a bushy moustache, singing as if he hadn't a care in the world.

'I mean, who's the cheerful guy?'

'Vince-Halliday. A great card. The Indian troops practically worship him. You know that we chased the Turks for over a hundred miles before the tide turned against us? Well, we were equipped for a short skirmish in India, not a full-scale bloody war in Mesopotamia. Vince-Halliday usually led the charge. You should see him'– revolver in one hand and a fly-whisk in the other – and a company of men with fixed bayonets following him into Turkish outposts. Then he got half his stomach blown away in the siege of Kut. None of us thought he'd survive, but he's a tough old bird.'

'Let us take it as it comes,' Vince-Halliday bellowed, right out of tune.

'Amen to that, brother,' said Holt, grinning.

'Look, you chaps!' Vince-Halliday shouted. 'Down the street!'

Holt, Birdie and the other officers rushed out on to the balconies overlooking the street. They saw a Turkish sergeant on a thin horse ambling up the street, the dust and stains of the desert on both. And behind him a tattered array of scarecrows whipped on by shouting Askars on mules.

'Poor bastards,' said Birdie. 'It's our men.'

Holt looked down horrified at what he saw.

'Look there!' said Captain Hyde-Dunning. 'That's Parks, isn't it?'

He called down to the shuffling column of prisoners.

'Sergeant Parks!'

A sun-burnt and scruffy face turned to stare up at the balcony. Parks was wearing the rags of a uniform but he still had his boots and was marching with more strength than the others.

Colonel Cottram came out on to the balcony to see what was happening.

'It's Sergeant Parks, sir,' said Hyde-Dunning. 'Second battalion. Do you remember him?'

'Yes, of course I do.'

'How are you shaping, sergeant?' Hyde-Dunning called.

'Bloody awful, sir,' Parks called back.

'What have your conditions been like?' Vince-Halliday asked, his face showing concern.

'Disgusting, sir. They treat us worse than animals.'

Holt fetched one of the bottles of beer from the zinc bath inside and called down.

'Sergeant – catch!'

He threw the cool bottle. It was a good throw, as the shuffling column had moved Parks fifteen yards down the street. But Parks was not expecting a bottle. He grabbed at it, but it hit his arm and smashed on the ground. He grimaced at Holt over his shoulder as he moved on.

The guards put the prisoners in a compound on the edge of town, gave them their meagre ration and water and left them to their own devices. Most of the men lay down and fell asleep as soon as they had eaten.

Not Parks. Ten years in the British army in India had taught him a trick or two. He sat himself in a doorway, back to the post, and got out his pack of cards. One of the Askars sidled over after a while, long whip dangling from his wrist, to see what he was doing. He watched, squinting in concentration as Parks demonstrated Find the Lady with three cards.

'There she is, in the middle,' the sergeant said, though the Askar understood not a word. 'Right? Now, I move the cards about like this, left over, right over, middle to left, right to the middle. And now where's the Lady? You think it's that one, mate, don't you? You're wrong. There she is.'

The Askar made him do it again, watching closely. Then he wanted to try it for himself, thinking that the cards themselves did the trick. He put out his hand for the cards. Parks nodded and held out his own hand.

After a brief pause, the Askar got the message. He pulled out of his pocket a thick slice of hard, black bread, part of his daily ration. He offered it to Parks.

Parks took the bread and let the Askar try with the cards. While the puzzled man was attempting to make the trick work, Parks broke the slice of bread into two, tucked one half inside his shirt and ate the other half. He had all the instincts to survive. And survival meant food. Some to eat now and some for later.

While Parks was struggling to keep himself alive, something was stirring in Holt up in the officers' billet. His own ill-treatment by the villagers and the killing of White had made a deep impression on him. But in retrospect he was able to see the whole dreadful episode as the ignorant rage of a savage and primitive tribe against a stranger. If someone from the next village had been brought in by the soldiers, he might well have been beaten the same way. Though that didn't make it any better, and if Holt had been able, he would have gladly led a punitive expedition back to the village.

But what he had seen that afternoon when the column came in was different. The human wreckage he had watched shuffling up the street under the Askars' whips were all that was left of a once well-trained and disciplined fighting-force. They had been deliberately broken in health and in spirit by the Turks. Nor was there any end in sight to their treatment – it was not very likely that the Turks would let them sit around a prison compound at Samarra for the rest of the war, however long that might be.

They would be moved on, for sure. They would be ill-treated and starved and beaten until even the strongest of them lay down and died, Holt feared. There was no use or place that he could see for large numbers of prisoners in this god-awful country. The Kut Column were walking dead men.

He found the chaplain sitting in the courtyard in the

29

pleasant evening air. The officers had finished dinner a little time before. The chaplain had an oil lamp on the table and was reading his bible.

Holt broached the subject in his mind.

'Sir, I think it's rotten, the way they're treating our guys out there. We've got to do something.'

The Moslem call to prayer wailed out over Samarra from the tallest minaret. The chaplain looked up from his book and shook his head sadly.

'They're all going to die, you know that,' Holt persisted.

Birdie drifted across the yard and joined them.

'Do you know your bible, Lieutenant Holt?' the chaplain asked.

'Some, sir. Why?'

'I wonder if you know this part I've just been reading: "Are not five sparrows sold for two farthings, and not one of them is forgotten before God? Even the very hairs on your head are numbered. Fear not, therefore, ye are of more value than many sparrows." '

The call of the faithful to prayer wailed out over the town again.

Holt cleared his throat to speak his mind, but Birdie got in first to prevent him.

'Remember Snell, chaplain? He used to keep little birds in India. Had a parrot as well and he taught it to speak.'

Colonel Cottram came into the yard from the street, a guard trailing along behind him. He stopped at the table and looked blankly at the officers there.

'Gentlemen,' he said. 'The commandant has just informed me that we shall be leaving here tomorrow morning. Find the adjutant, Birdie and send him to me. There's a lot to arrange.'

'You mean all of us, sir?' Holt queried. 'Officers and other ranks?'

'The officers are being moved. I was given no information about the plans for the men.'

He went away, leaving Holt thinking. But there was nothing much he could do. Packing was no problem, since

30

he owned nothing except the clothes he had bought in the bazaar to replace those stolen from him when he was captured. What the hell the colonel and the adjutant had to arrange, he couldn't imagine. He decided to turn in.

In the morning the officers paraded in the courtyard early, orderlies with them to take care of their kit. But it was half-way through the morning before the Turks got themselves organised to move them. A battered convoy of ancient lorries and cars wheezed down the street and stopped outside their billet.

To his horror, Holt found himself pushed by an uncomprehending Turk into the lead car with Colonel Cottram and Major Pett, while the vehicles behind were filled with other officers, their kit, their orderlies and three armed guards.

'Sorry about this, sir,' he apologised to the colonel. 'That guy just heaved me in here. I'll go back into one of the lorries.'

'Sit still, Mr Holt,' said the colonel stiffly.

Down at the bonnet, an Arab was furiously swinging the starting-handle. When he stopped from exhaustion, the engine hadn't even coughed.

The colonel looked at Holt.

'I suppose you only know about planes, not cars?'

'All engines are much the same, sir. I could take a look under the bonnet.'

'Certainly not!' Major Pett barked. 'We're passengers, Holt, not mechanics.'

Birdie Partridge, who had learned the ways of their captors, came drifting along the convoy carrying half a dozen umbrellas with tassels.

'Still here, sir?' he asked the colonel cheerfully. 'I just nipped into the bazaar for some last-minute shopping. Didn't think I'd miss the bus.'

'What have you got there, Birdie?'

The lieutenant offered a Turkish umbrella to the colonel. 'Thought we'd need something to keep the sun off, sir. It's going to be pretty fierce by noon. Have one of these, sir – only five piastres.'

The adjutant glared at him.

'Mr Partridge, there is a paragraph in King's Regulations which states that a British officer will not carry an umbrella unless in civilian clothes. Are you familiar with it?'

Birdie's face fell. The colonel came to his rescue.

'I'm sure they're very effective. Give them to the orderlies to put with our kit, there's a good chap.'

'And bear in mind that we are British officers, not members of a Chinese tight-rope act,' the adjutant growled.

'Yes, sir,' said Birdie, and scurried away.

It seemed to Holt that Birdie's suggestion had been a practical one and was probably inspired by some kind of protective feeling for the colonel, who looked frailer and more defeated with each passing day. Major Pett was stupid to knock him down like that.

The Arab swung the handle again and the engine burst into life, wheezing and knocking.

'About time,' said Pett, looking at his watch. 'Bloody in-efficient lot, the Turks.'

So where's the hurry, Holt thought, we're not going any-where important. But he said nothing.

The lead car rolled down the street and the convoy followed it noisily. Vince-Halliday could be heard roaring out his song about life being full of plums, but nobody else joined in.

Out of Samarra and its outskirts, the road became a beaten earth track and before long they were out in the wilderness again, crossing a huge waste of nothing. History said this had once been a fertile and prosperous land. Together Arabs and Turks had reduced it to little short of desert. Holt discovered the advantage of being in the lead car. The dust they stirred up floated back over the convoy, making the passengers splutter and cough, and even shutting up Vince-Halliday.

They bounced on across the barren and brutal landscape, wondering where they were going and when they would arrive. And there was another nasty reminder waiting for them down the dirt track.

Though the motorised column had taken until half-way through the morning to get going, the Turks had whipped the other ranks out of the compound and got them on the march at first light. Five or six miles from Samarra, Holt saw the trudging column ahead.

As the convoy caught up, the lead car driver honked his vast bulb horn. The Askars yelled and cracked their whips to drive the prisoners off the track to let the vehicles pass. And as it passed, it submerged the column in a cloud of heavy dust that added to the men's misery.

Holt gripped the side of the sun-blistered car and stared at the men. He saw whip-marked backs, bare and bleeding feet, faces without hope.

He looked at the colonel, hoping for some response. But the colonel stared straight ahead, pale and unseeing.

He's going to crack, Holt thought. The man's at the end of his tether. He's no use anymore, poor bastard.

He looked at Major Pett. The adjutant's face was fiery red and his jaw was clenched.

Well, at least he feels something, Holt decided. But he's no use either. He's just a bull-neck. Nothing inside his head except King's Regulations, and they don't cover this situation.

He looked back at the column and through the swirling dust saw an Askar off his mule flogging a prisoner who had collapsed and could not get up. Then he looked away, not wanting to see the end of it.

3

Chapter 4

The convoy came at last to an old mud-walled fort, built long ago by the Turks to house a garrison to keep the Arabs in check. By the look of its fortifications, it dated from the days when the Turks were equipped with flintlock rifles and the natives with swords. Even a small field gun would have demolished it in ten minutes. Over the years a small shanty town had grown up round the fort's walls.

God, thought Holt, I've seen some one-eyed dumps in my time but this looks like the end of the line.

The orderlies off-loaded the officers' kit while the colonel was escorted to the commandant's office. The rest of them sat around in the main yard of the fort in the shade, exchanging idle chatter and useless speculation.

'I suppose you feel at home, here, old boy,' Captain Hyde-Dunning said to Holt. 'Just like your Wild West, isn't it?'

'No, sir,' said Holt, grinning. 'There's not a town in the West without a saloon. And I don't see one here.'

That got a laugh.

It was some time before the colonel came back. They stood as he approached.

'Well, sir?' the adjutant asked.

'The commandant here is called Muzloom Bey. Fellow looks like a fat pig and speaks no English at all. But as far as I can make out through his interpreter his attitude is a fairly civil one. This is Fort Mosul and here we stay for the duration.'

34

Holt and Birdie exchanged dismayed looks. Fort Mosul looked a terrible place to sit out the rest of the war.

'The other officers taken at Kut will be joining us here from time to time, as and when the Turks can find transport to get them here. We shall be a community of about four hundred eventually, and there's plenty of accommodation here in the fort. The men will follow the same route as we did, in columns of two or three hundred at a time. Some have already passed through. They will be taken on in a north-westerly direction to wherever it is they're being taken. I could get no information on that score.'

'I say!' Birdie exclaimed softly.

'You will each be issued with a postcard to send home to your next of kin,' the colonel continued. 'It will take months to get home but at least you can tell your family that you are safe and well. The cards will be censored by the Turks so don't bother with descriptions of where you think you are or what is happening to the men. They'll simply tear your card up if you try that.'

Holt grunted in disgust.

'You will also be given a parole form to sign,' said the colonel. 'This will be your written guarantee that you will not attempt to escape. Since we are stuck in the middle of nowhere, surrounded by hostile natives, there is no point whatsoever in attempting to escape. You would be dead inside twenty-four hours at the most, either from the natives or from the sun. I therefore urge you to sign the parole form and make life a lot easier for everybody. We shall then be given a fair measure of freedom of movement in the fort and in the village.'

'Are you ordering us to sign, sir?' Holt asked, wanting to have the position clear.

'No, Mr Holt, I have no authority to order you to sign such a form, since it is your duty as laid down in King's Regulations to escape from enemy hands if an opportunity presents itself. But as you cannot escape, you are not bound by that. I am urging you to sign, not ordering you.'

Everything the colonel said confirmed Holt's view that he

35

had reached the end of his tether and was not functioning as a commanding officer. But there was no point in arguing in public.

'I'm not sure about the position in regard to pay,' said the colonel. 'The Turks do not intend to feed us. Muzloom Bey appeared to say that he had no funds here to pay us, which may mean no more than that he has appropriated the money himself. However, I am given to understand that there is a merchant in the village who will accept written promissory notes from you in return for cash. He has some means of collecting from your banks in England, no doubt through a neutral country. You will get a wretched rate of exchange, I imagine – not more than a shilling in the pound. But at least it shows that an Englishman's word is accepted as practically sacred even in these parts, which is encouraging. Right, I think that's about it.'

'If I may, sir?' said Major Pett briskly.

'Carry on.'

The major addressed them.

'We've put up a notice board in my billet and the chaplain has posted details of church parade on Sunday. Other notices will be put there and I strongly advise each of you to make a point of reading the board every morning.'

'Great,' Holt muttered to Birdie. 'That's just what we needed – a notice board with details of church parade.'

When they were dismissed, they went to explore their quarters – a succession of empty earth-floored rooms inside the fort.

'Not exactly the Ritz,' said Birdie. 'But if we buy a few rush mats and get our bed-rolls down, it will at least be habitable. And if we're stuck here until the war's over, we have to make the best of it.'

'The hell with that,' said Holt. 'I'm not staying in this flea-hole a day longer than I have to.'

'But . . .' said Birdie, sounding distressed. 'You're not going to try to escape, old boy? I mean, what the colonel said was right, you know – there's absolutely nowhere to go to from here. You will sign the parole form, won't you?'

36

'No promises,' said Holt. 'I might build an aeroplane out of tent-poles and goat-skin and fly out.'

Birdie laughed.

Later in the day Holt saw something which convinced him finally that the British officers were totally insane. In the cool of the late afternoon he found Vince-Halliday and a couple of others out on the old parade ground. Vince-Halliday was holding a six foot pole and dipping the end into a tin of red dye.

'What are you doing, Captain? Putting up a flag-pole so we can salute the flag every morning?'

'Pig-sticking, old man,' Vince-Halliday said, smiling. 'After polo it's the best sport we have in India. Well, tiger shooting's pretty good, of course.'

'Pig-sticking? I've read about it but I've never seen it. What do you do?'

'Simple. Parts of India are full of wild pig. Big bristly things with tusks six inches long. The beaters drive one out of where it's hiding in the long grass and you chase it on horseback with a cavalry lance. The idea is to stick it and kill it.'

'Sounds pretty simple,' said Holt.

'He's having you on,' Birdie explained. 'They're a bit fierce, wild pig. And you're hunting them over broken ground. If your horse falls or throws you, there's a good chance the pig will turn and have a go at you. They're not afraid of a man on foot. You can get quite badly cut about. Chaps have been killed, in fact.'

'So where's the wild pig here?'

Vince-Halliday grinned.

'I bought it in the village this afternoon. Only got one, but I thought it would provide a bit of fun. I'm not going to spear it – only chase it. The red dye will show where I score a hit.'

'Is he joking?' Holt asked Birdie.

'Good Lord, no. We both felt the need for a spot of exercise and then we spotted this porker. Stand well back when the fun starts – we don't want you to get knocked over.'

Vince-Halliday had bought, or borrowed, a scraggy donkey. He swung a leg over its back and took the reins in his left hand, his red-tipped pole tucked under his right arm.

'Ready?' he shouted across the parade ground.

'Ready!' Hyde-Dunning shouted back.

'Right – let him go!'

Captain Hyde-Dunning released a small pig which ran squealing across the parade ground. Vince-Halliday kicked his heels into the donkey's sides and urged it into a shambling trot in pursuit of the piglet. He was shouting blood-curdling cries in Hindi as he chased the frightened and squealing pig.

Holt roared with laughter at the spectacle of a British officer engaged in so ludicrous a pastime. Vince-Halliday was crazy, and Birdie too. But he liked them both. The rest of the officers were equally crazy, but not all in the same friendly way.

After a chase of a few minutes, Vince-Halliday cornered the pig by the wall and poked at him with his pole.

'Got him!'

He rode over to Holt and dismounted.

'Have a go,' he said, offering the pole. 'See if you like the sport. Used to do a lot of it in India before we came to this bloody awful country. Had better mounts, of course.'

Shaking his head in wonderment, Holt clambered on to the donkey and found that his feet touched ground on either side. He tucked them up behind him against the donkey's flanks, took a good grip on the 'lance' and urged his steed into motion.

Birdie began to shout advice as Holt bore down on the panting piglet.

'Make him run and stick him from behind – under the left shoulder. You can see where Vince marked him – that's the spot. Straight into the heart!'

The pig roused itself and set off across the parade ground at a fast speed. Holt pulled the donkey's head round and kicked it to get it moving faster. The donkey froze on rigid legs in protest and Holt sailed over its head.

He landed with a bump that knocked him breathless for a

second. Then he looked up to see the donkey standing behind him, showing its yellow teeth as if laughing at him.

Meanwhile the piglet had reached the opposite side of the parade ground, turned and was coming back, squealing, straight at Holt sitting on the ground.

'Get up, man!' Vince-Halliday shouted in mock alarm.

'Wild pig coming for you!' Birdie chortled.

Holt scrambled up and got back on to the donkey's back. The little pig ran right underneath the donkey and went squealing off into the distance.

'Lost your spear, man,' Vince-Halliday called. 'Only thing to do in that situation is clear out quick.'

Holt walked the donkey over to them.

'Like your first taste of pig-sticking?' Birdie asked, straight-faced.

'The hell with it. I'll take polo instead.'

It was late the next day when the column of prisoners staggered into Fort Mosul. The officers watched in silence as the men were herded by the Askars into a barbed wire enclosure outside the fort. It seemed to Holt that there were fewer of them than he had seen back at Samarra.

He went to see the adjutant, but was sent away abruptly as soon as he started to speak.

Morosely he went back to the officers' quarters. To his disgust he found Vince-Halliday feeding his tethered pig on a bowl of mash as if it were a prize pet.

'Did you see the column when it came in?' Holt demanded angrily. 'Did you see the shape they were in?'

Vince-Halliday scratched the pig behind its ears as it gobbled its food.

'I suppose you're thinking that they'd be glad to have Porky's supper. Is that what's bothering you?'

'I don't understand any of you. I tried to talk to Major Pett and got nowhere. All I did was point out that they're still our men and we're still their officers.'

'Well, well,' Vince-Halliday grinned. 'I'm damn sure you got nowhere. Major Pett has been in the army for fifteen years. He doesn't take kindly to having things pointed out to

39

him by subalterns with less than six months' service.'

'I guess it's because I'm not British,' Holt muttered.

'No, give him credit for more sense than that. He's as angry as you are but he knows there's nothing he can do about it, so he doesn't care to be reminded of the situation.'

'Just who says we can't do anything about it?'

'In the Turkish language, old boy, the word for prisoner and the word for slave is the same. That gives you an idea of their thinking and explains why our men are getting the treatment that is infuriating us all.'

Holt glared at him.

'I don't need a lesson in Turkish, sir.'

Vince-Halliday did not take offence.

'Officers are a privileged class, Holt.'

'Sure, but we have responsibilities as well.'

'Fine phrases, Lieutenant. What are you going to do about it?'

'Why don't we sneak down into that compound and talk with the men. We could present their grievances to the commandant and make him listen.'

'Damned tricky getting down into that compound.'

'What about bribing one of the guards to take us there? They'll do about anything for money.'

'I've just tried,' said Vince-Halliday. 'No go, old boy. They've been given special orders to keep officers away from the prisoner compound, under threat of a real flogging. So bribery's not on. But there may be another way.'

Holt looked at him in surprise.

'Go and get Mr Vallance and Mr Partridge. You'll find them waiting in their room.'

He unrolled a blanket and Holt saw the contents. Strips of cloth torn to make bandages, bottles of oil, bread and three pairs of Turkish shoes.

'Great, sir,' said Holt. 'I've got a bottle of local hooch. Shall I bring it?'

'Good idea. Hurry up and get the others.'

Vallance and Birdie Partridge were waiting and ready, each equipped with stuff bought in the village. Back upstairs in Vince-Halliday's room, they watched him tie one end of a rope round his waist and the other round his bundle. He sat astride the window ledge.

'I'll tug on the rope when I'm up. If everything's all right, tug back and I'll haul the bundle up and let the rope down again for you to follow me.'

'Right, sir,' said Birdie eagerly. 'But why don't you let me go first? I mean, you're still pretty well on the sick list.'

'Don't argue, Birdie. I'm senior officer here and I shall go first. When you come after me, keep quiet. We don't want a sentry to hear us and get nervous. He might take a pot-shot at us and then the game's up.'

They watched him climb up on the outside of the window ledge and shin upwards to the flat roof above.

'You go next, Birdie,' Vallance said, using his seniority. 'Keep close to Vince up there and watch him. He's not really well enough for this sort of lark and we don't want him falling off the roof and breaking his neck. Holt, you follow Birdie. I'll bring up the rear and keep an eye out for sentries and such. If you hear me whistle once, lie flat and stay still. Two short whistles for all clear. Got it? Up you go, Birdie.'

Up on the roof they made their way cautiously round to the side of the fort nearest the compound. Vince-Halliday had tied the end of his rope round a rafter showing through cracked tiles. He dropped the rope over the wall and turned to climb down backwards.

'Hold on,' said Vallance. 'Let me go first and do a recce. You're in charge of the sortie, Vince, so you need a situation report before you commit the whole force.'

Before Vince-Halliday could protest, Vallance swung himself over the edge and shinned down the rope into the darkness below. The three of them crouched and waited until there was a tug on the rope.

'Right, I'll go next,' Vince-Halliday said quickly. 'You two follow as quick as you can. Once on the ground, stay in the shadows and move sharp.'

They got to the compound without being challenged. It was no problem to crawl in under the wire. They found a sorry sight – men sprawled out on the ground in exhaustion, fever and disease.

Vallance lit a small oil-lamp he had brought.

'Good God,' he said. 'Where on earth shall we start? We need a field hospital to look after all the casualties here.'

'We'll have to make do with what we've got,' said Vince-Halliday grimly. 'Look out, here comes a guard. Holt, you keep him busy.'

An Arab guard made his way across the compound, attracted by the lamp. He was talking officiously as he came, probably demanding to know what was going on, though none of them could understand him.

Holt pulled out his bottle of raki, uncorked it and took a quick swig. It tasted like fire-water. He coughed and shuddered.

'My God, make good antiseptic if you want it.'

He went to meet the guard, talking cheerfully and holding out his bottle.

'Try a drop of this. Go on – do you a world of good.'

The guard glared at him suspiciously, half unslinging his rifle from his shoulder. Holt took another swig to demonstrate what he meant and then stuffed the neck of the bottle into the guard's mouth.

The Arab took a long swig. As he lowered the bottle, his eyes watering, Holt slipped a few coins into his hand.

'Little present for not bothering us. OK?'

The guard opened his mouth to say something, but Holt put an arm round his shoulders and led him away from the circle of lamplight, talking in a friendly voice.

'Come on, you ugly little bastard,' he said. 'Get back to your post and leave us alone.'

He took the guard all the way back to the gate. When he got back to the lamplight, he found that Vallance had set up an improvised sickbay.

'Right, chaps,' said Vince-Halliday. 'Vallance will do the first aid bit. He's good at that. The rest of us will move quietly through the men and find the ones most in need of treatment and get them to Vallance. Don't start with the

42

merely desperate – pick the ones that look as if they won't last the night. We'll go back for the others later, if we have time.'

They went about their task with the minimum of disturbance, so as not to attract any more guards.

Holt helped two or three of the worst-looking cases over to Vallance, who was kneeling on the ground, his rag bandages and other equipment laid out by him. It seemed to Holt sensible to start with the men whose feet were in worst condition for marching – they were the ones who would fall out of the column first.

Over near the door of a mud-wall building he was surprised to find Sergeant Parks hunched over a tiny fire, stirring something in a pot and sniffing at it.

'You look all right, Sergeant,' said Holt sharply. 'How about lending a hand?'

'And have my supper stolen by some poor starving bastard?'

'Damn your supper, man. There's work to be done.'

Before the argument could go any further, Vince-Halliday materialised out of the darkness beside Holt.

'Mr Holt, look after those men over there by the wire. They've got dysentery, I think, and they're lying in their own muck because they're too weak to do anything about it. See if you can clean them up a bit.'

Holt did as he was bid. His stomach heaved and he could hardly prevent himself from retching at the stench that came off the half dozen men lying on the ground. One of them was moaning quietly and another was muttering the Lord's Prayer.

He had no idea what to do for the best. Before he could decide, he heard Vince-Halliday call out sharply.

'Birdie – bring me a knife – quick!'

The urgency in his voice made Holt leave the men he had been told to help and hurry over to see what was the matter. Vince-Halliday had found two men, both Indians, tied hand and foot and stripped naked, lying face down.

Birdie handed him a knife and he cut one man loose. The

43

man was shuddering and muttering under his breath in his own language. Vince-Halliday cut the other man's bonds and turned him over. Then he let out a shout of rage as he recognised him.

'Why were they tied like that?' Holt asked.

'Don't know,' Birdie muttered. 'Think the guards assaulted them. You know – no money to pay for a woman. That's Ranji – he was Vince's bearer.'

There was shouting over by the compound gate. Feeling sick from what he had just been told, Holt looked that way and saw a Turkish corporal and half a dozen guards heading towards them. The guard he had tried to bribe had no doubt alerted them.

'Trouble on the way,' he said to Vince-Halliday.

The captain did not hear him. He was bending over the emaciated Indian youth on the ground.

'My poor Ranji,' he said. 'What have the bastards done to you?'

The guards surrounded them and were shouting furiously now that they saw the officers in the prisoner compound. Vince-Halliday got slowly to his feet. He stared briefly at the Turkish corporal and, to Holt's amazement, flattened him with a smashing right hook.

The guards jumped in to grab Vince-Halliday. With a shout of pure pleasure at action at last, Holt waded in with both fists. After a moment's startled pause, Birdie joined in as well. One or two of the fitter soldiers nearby came into the fight, overjoyed at the chance of landing one on the guards who had ill-treated them for so long. Holt was in his element, letting all his pent-up frustration out in the punches he landed on yelling guards.

But it didn't last long. Alerted by the noise, more guards came pouring in and separated the two sides with whips and gun-butts.

Vallance, Birdie and Holt were overpowered roughly and dragged away. Vince-Halliday was unconscious on the ground. Two of the guards picked him up and brought him along.

They were taken to the commandant's office and stood licking their wounds while Colonel Cottram was sent for. The commandant did indeed look like a pig, as the colonel had said. He was fat and had slitty eyes and a turned-up nose. He shouted abuse in Turkish at the four officers until Colonel Cottram arrived.

The colonel took in the scene at a glance: three of his officers looking the worse for wear; Captain Vince-Halliday slumped on a chair looking more dead than alive.

He faced the commandant bleakly and demanded to know what was going on and why British officers were being beaten.

The commandant's aide was the only one who spoke English. He was very young, slender and olive-skinned, almost girlishly pretty.

'Muzloom Bey is angry,' he said. 'These officers were in the prisoner compound, where they should not be. When the guards asked them why they were there, they beat the guards. This is not correct behaviour for a British officer.'

'A British officer looks after his men,' Vince-Halliday said feebly from his chair. 'Those men are sick and starving.'

The aide translated for the commandant and waited for his answer.

'Muzloom Bey says it is not your concern. They are prisoners.'

'Why the hell don't you feed them?' Vince-Halliday demanded.

'They are fed every day,' the aide said, looking puzzled.

'A handful of slops – is that what you call feeding?'

'Be silent, Mr Vince-Halliday,' Colonel Cottram ordered.

'I will not be silent, sir. It's disgraceful!'

'I am giving you a direct order.'

Shaid the aide had exchanged comments with the commandant.

'Muzloom Bey does not understand your complaint. All your men are given the same daily ration as our own soldiers.'

The British officers exchanged looks of amazement and

doubt. Muzloom Bey spoke angrily and Shaid translated.

'All British officers will parade for the commandant at dawn tomorrow.'

'Get Captain Vince-Halliday to his quarters,' the colonel ordered Birdie and Holt. 'I shall have something to say to you tomorrow after the parade.'

Vince-Halliday grunted in pain as they lifted him from his chair. He had been knocked about badly in the fight and clearly was injured internally.

Holt and Birdie carried him to his quarters and put him to bed.

'Anything you need?' Holt asked.

'Not really. Just a bath, clean clothes, a square meal and a bottle of champagne.'

'Room service has gone off duty for the night,' said Holt, smiling briefly at Vince-Halliday's determination not to give in. 'Will tomorrow be all right?'

'Very well. But I shall complain to the management of this hotel.'

'Try to get some sleep,' Birdie advised.

'Sorry I didn't get that guard squared properly to leave us alone,' Holt apologised.

'Never mind, old boy. I enjoyed the scrap while it lasted.'

Chapter 5

It was still dark when the orderlies woke the officers. They shaved by oil-lamp and made themselves as respectable as they could before hurrying down to the parade ground. By custom, the Indian officers formed their ranks a little apart from the British. The half dozen orderlies formed a separate squad.

Two of the orderlies had been bandsmen and one of them still had his drum with the regimental battle-honours lettered on it in gold. Birdie Partridge, eternal public schoolboy, brought his euphonium on parade with him and took charge of the squad of orderlies.

Vince-Halliday was too weak to stand and should not have been there at all. He insisted on joining the parade, as he felt responsible for it. He sat awkwardly on his donkey, legs trailing on the ground. He was very obviously in pain.

The senior officer called them to attention as Colonel Cottram marched on to the parade ground, followed at a distance of three paces by Major Pett.

The colonel took his place at the head of his officers. The adjutant shouted an order and they marched smartly on to the parade ground, followed by Vince-Halliday on his shambling mount, then the band led by Birdie and then the Indian officers.

Marching with the British officers, Holt straightened his back and his face. He had to hand it to them – come hell or high water, with all their faults, the British intended to put on a show for their own benefit.

Vince-Halliday's voice was raised in a cracked song to the rhythm of drum and euphonium. Not the proper words, but the words the enlisted men sang when they were marching at ease.

'We won't be buggered about,
We won't be buggered about . . . '

Major Pett, furious at the impropriety of an officer singing on parade bellowed over his shoulder.

'Silence in the ranks!'

Vince-Halliday ignored him.

'Wherever we go we always shout
We're buggered if we'll be buggered about . . . '

'Silence!' the adjutant shouted again.

The whole parade took up the song with Vince-Halliday at that. Holt had not heard the words before but he caught on quickly and sang with gusto.

'We won't be buggered about,
Wherever we go we always shout . . . '

'Parade . . . halt! Right . . . turn!'

The music and singing stopped instantly. Each man stood smartly to attention, shoulders back and eyes to the front, arms straight down, under the balcony of Muzloom Bey's room.

The Turk came out and surveyed the ranks imperiously from his balcony. Shaid at his side had dark patches under his eyes, as if the commandant had given him a hard night.

Colonel Cottram took three paces forward and saluted.

'Eight British officers, one sick, four Indian officers, six orderlies, all present and correct, sir,' he reported.

Muzloom Bey touched the side of his head with the short whip in his hand by way of returning the salute. He addressed the parade at some length in Turkish.

Shaid translated.

'The commandant is glad that you are content and that you sing your regimental song for him.'

There were one or two guffaws, quickly suppressed when Major Pett turned to glare at the offenders.

'Muzloom Bey says there will be no more fighting by you.

The compound where the ordinary soldiers are kept is out of bounds to all officers, otherwise they are breaking their word, which among gentlemen is not done. He says there will be no punishments this time because he likes you and respects you all. But if such things happen again, he will make discipline so that you will remember. You may dismiss.'

After the parade, Holt, Birdie and Vallance were summoned to the colonel's quarters. Major Pett was with him, looking as furious with the world as ever. Vince-Halliday had been put back to bed.

'Stand to attention,' the adjutant ordered.

The colonel spoke to the point.

'On this occasion I shall excuse the three of you because you were obviously led on by Captain Vince-Halliday. I'm sorry that he's now suffering the consequences of his action. I know what he feels about the terrible conditions our men are having to suffer. Dammit, we all feel the same about it. But nobody, not even Vince-Halliday, for whom I have the greatest respect as an officer, nobody can be a law to himself, whatever his motives. Is that understood?'

'Yes, sir,' they chorused.

'Very well. I must insist that you do not break your parole again. You must leave it to me to keep in touch with Muz-loom Bey regarding the well-being of the other ranks.'

'Sir,' said Vallance. 'There's already talk about moving them on. Can't the sick be left here till they're fitter? A third of them are riddled with dysentery and in no state to march.'

'I don't believe the commandant will agree to anything like that, but I shall continue to try. You've seen for yourself what sort of a man he is and so you know what to expect.'

'But, sir,' Vallance tried again, ignoring Major Pett's stony gaze. 'Some of the men said that they think they're on a death march.'

'And what is that?'

'They believe they're going to be marched up and down this awful country on filthy rations and with no medical assistance until every one of them drops dead.'

'I can't believe that. If the Turks intended to kill them,

they'd simply shoot them on the spot and be done with it. We've seen enough evidence of that.'

'The fact is, sir, that most of the men are unfit to march. We saw that for ourselves last night. And some of the things we heard about the way they'd been treated – '

The adjutant cut him off short.

'Mr Holt, you are a foreigner and therefore cannot be expected to understand. The British regular soldier is the salt of the earth. He loves to grumble – that shows his spirit. But when he's put to the test, he can take a lot as well as give it. He's been trained for it. If you had served as long with him as I have, you'd know that he is well able to look after himself.'

It was too much for Holt.

'Sir, why are you talking about *the* British soldier? You keep referring to *him* as if there were only one of them. They're individuals. A lot of them have already died on their way here from Kut and a lot more are going to die when they're moved on again. Some of the men in that compound are going to die in the next couple of days. And they know it. They've given up hope.'

Colonel Cottram answered him.

'Major Pett referred to *the* British soldier because he *is* a type. Each one has the same traditions behind him – traditions which equip him to make the absolute best of whatever circumstances he finds himself in.'

'I see,' said Holt, furious at being fobbed off. 'And just what tradition equips him to get over dysentery?'

Major Pett eyed him coldly.

'If a man's got dysentery, there's nothing anybody can do about it, not even you, Mr Holt.'

Holt wasn't having that.

'They've only got dysentery because they're not bloody well being looked after and you know it.'

Colonel Cottram thought it best to stop this young and excitable officer from going any further with the adjutant.

'Mr Holt, when we were forced by starvation to surrender at Kut, General Townshend personally promised the men that he would negotiate with the Turks to ensure they got fair treatment.'

'Then the general's failed, hasn't he?' said Holt.

Birdie and Vallance looked to their front, away from Holt's flushed face and the stony paleness of the colonel.

'You will retract that remark, Mr Holt,' said the colonel, his voice frozen with shock at the disrespect from a subaltern to a senior officer. 'And if there is any more of this sort of thing from you, I'll have you placed under close arrest and confined to your quarters. I've made all the allowances I'm going to make for you because you are not a British officer and don't fully understand our way of doing things. From now on you will simply obey orders, whether you understand them or not. Is that clear?'

There was no mistaking the tone. Holt stood to attention and said:

'Sir.'

'One thing more, Holt, you are the only one of my officers who has not yet signed the parole form and returned it to the adjutant. I want it in his hands immediately.'

'Sir.'

'I don't know what hare-brained notions you might be harbouring about escape, but I shall repeat what I said earlier as a point of information and you will now take it as an order. This is the fortress town of Mosul and here we stay. Got it?'

'Sir.'

Holt knew that in the British army to say 'Sir' meant 'Yes, sir.' To Holt it meant no such thing. It signified only that he had heard the order and had understood it. It did not necessarily signify compliance. Holt intended to take what action seemed best to him personally.

In Francis Holt's highly individual view, fostered by his American background and upbringing, a sensible man only took orders from a commander who demonstrated that he had a grip on the situation and knew what he was doing. Neither Colonel Cottram nor Major Pett fitted into that category, as far as he was concerned.

He saw them as losers who had given up fighting and were planning to sit out the rest of the war in whatever meagre comfort they could organise for themselves in this flea-bitten ragbag of a clapped-out fort.

In Holt's book there was nothing to be achieved by taking orders from losers. That wasn't what they'd taught him at military academy.

Sure, the colonel and Pett might have a bad conscience about the men and what was happening to them. But they were passing the buck by telling themselves that there was nothing they could do about it. And that was exactly what they were going to do about it – nothing.

Holt didn't give in that easily. Plans were revolving in his head as he saluted the colonel and left him.

Chapter 6

As long as a guard went with them, the officers were allowed to wander about the village and the dusty land outside as they wished. Muzloom Bey knew there was nowhere for them to go and had no fear of escape attempts.

After the midday heat cooled into early evening Holt and Birdie went for a walk. Birdie was pathetically anxious to hang on to Holt. He was only a couple of years older but he admired the American for his spirit in standing up to senior officers and speaking his mind.

Poor Birdie, trained in the English public school tradition and commissioned into the Indian army at eighteen, was incapable of arguing with a senior officer or questioning an order.

Good but limited, was Holt's assessment of him. Put Birdie in front of a platoon of men and order him to lead a bayonet charge against ten times his own number and he'd do it without blinking. And if he got hit, he'd die bravely without complaining. That was the way he saw his duty.

Holt tried to explain some of the American tradition, built on the frontier spirit when a man carried his own life in his hands and aimed at being self sufficient. He described the fierce discipline at the academy, when future officers were put through mental and physical punishment that sorted out the ones who weren't going to make it very early on.

'But after that, when you've passed out and have a command, you don't take orders without thinking about them.

Hell, we're all free men, even the enlisted men. A company commander expects some input from his junior officers and some initiative. What the hell are they trained for, otherwise?'

It was beyond Birdie's comprehension how an army could function like that. Holt gave up trying to explain.

They sat on top of a ridge of high ground outside Mosul, from where they could see the whole surrounding countryside. A flat, featureless nothing. They could see the whole of the fort and the village round it, and the compound where the prisoners were kept. The guards round the wire had been doubled to make sure no more officers got in to cause trouble.

'I say,' Birdie exclaimed joyfully. 'Look at those chaps.'

The other officers had marked out a pitch on the dusty ground outside the walls and were playing a ball game. Faintly in the distance Holt heard a voice cry, 'Well hit, sir!'

'Baseball?'

'Good Lord, no. Cricket, old boy. Have you ever played?'

'No. Looks like baseball from up here. What happens?'

'The bowler bowls to the batsman – that's Vallance down there – and he hits it. Then the batsman makes runs by changing ends while the fielders get the ball back to the wicket and try to run them out. Or you can be caught out. Not a bit like your game, as I understand it. That's like the game children play at home – rounders, we call it.'

'Looks a lot slower than baseball,' said Holt, amused.

A shadow fell across the pair of them. They turned, thinking it was the guard wanting them to go back to the fort. But the guard was ten paces away, sprawled on the ground and half-asleep.

It was Shaid, the Turkish commandant's aide.

He came and sat by them, a smile on his pretty face.

'What is they do, your comrades?' he asked.

'It's a game,' Birdie explained. 'We call it cricket. Do you play games like that in Turkey?'

Shaid smiled again and shook his head.

'Games with sticks and ball are for little boys,' he said

54

slyly. 'We have other games when we grow up.'

'Really?' said Birdie. 'Polo, you mean?'

Shaid laughed aloud.

'No, no, real games.'

'I'm blessed if I follow you,' said Birdie.

'You must forgive that I do not speak your language perfect, so it is difficult for me to explain as I am not understanding the right words. Do you speak French? I am very good in French.'

'Not very well, old boy. Only what I remember from school. How about you, Holt?'

'Never learned it.'

'I try,' said Shaid, smiling at them again. 'You are sometimes *couche à gauche* like the French say?'

'Sorry, old lad. I don't comprehend. No comprehend.'

Shaid giggled like a girl.

'You go with woman when you can to the bed, yes?'

'I say! One doesn't talk about that sort of thing, you know!'

'Maybe not talk, but do,' Shaid suggested.

'Sure,' said Holt, grinning and thinking to himself that it had been a hell of a long time since he got his ashes hauled.

'Are you telling us there's tail to be had in that dump down there?' he asked.

'Please?' said Shaid, puzzled by the words.

'In the village. Women?'

'But of course. Everywhere.'

'Is that what *couche à gauche* means?'

'No. It means to do with boy what you do with woman. You like that?'

'Really!' said Birdie, outraged. 'What a suggestion!'

Shaid did not take offence.

'You like to smoke opium? It is very friendly, very pleasant time. There is a place at the other end of town we could go. I show you. You are my friends.'

Holt was suddenly thoughtful.

'The other end of town is out of bounds to us because of what happened in the compound. We can't go there.'

55

'You are my guests. It can be arranged. I invite you, though I have no money to pay.'

That was why he had approached them.

'Don't give it a thought, Shaid,' said Holt. 'We've got money. We'll pay for everything.'

Shaid's face was wreathed in smiles.

'We have pleasant time, I promise. I call for you this evening. What time?'

'After mess,' said Holt. 'About nine.'

Shaid nodded and drifted away.

'Now look here,' said Birdie. 'You're not seriously intending to visit the local brothel with that awful little squirt, are you?'

'He can get us into the compound, Birdie, without all the fuss we had before. One word from him and the guards will stand back and salute us as we go in.'

'Never thought of that.'

'Right. So let's get down to the bazaar and buy some stuff to take with us for the men. And if we have to buy that little faggot a piece of ass to get us past the wire, so what? It'll be well worth it.'

They called to the guard to wake him and made their way back in a hurry.

In the bazaar they bought as much useful stuff as they thought they could manage, signing notes promising to pay later. And after the evening meal with the other officers they retired to the room they shared to get packed. They had a couple of bottles of olive oil, cloth for bandages, oranges and quite a lot of hard black bread. They were so engrossed that they failed to hear the adjutant come into the room.

'Birdie, Captain Hyde-Dunning has managed to make a presentable pack of playing cards,' Major Pett said, ignoring Holt. 'Will you make a fourth at bridge?'

He saw what they had laid out and the significance of it dawned on him. His face flushed dark red. Holt tackled him head-on.

'Look, sir, I'm going down to the compound. Birdie can please himself.'

The adjutant found his voice.

56

'Lieutenant Holt – I thought the colonel had made himself clear this morning.'

Birdie tried to pacify him.

'We were coming to ask your permission first, sir,' he lied.

'Be silent, Mr Partridge,' Major Putt thundered. 'Mr Holt, I realise that you are not Indian army like the rest of us, but surely you have some sense of your place and your duty?'

'I thought an officer's place was with his men, sir.'

Major Pett gobbled for some moments, then got himself under control. He spoke to Holt as if he were sentencing him to be taken out and shot against the nearest wall.

'An officer's place is something you are obviously unable to fill, Holt. How dare you speak to me like that! I have served in three campaigns.'

'And lost the last one,' Holt threw at him.

Birdie tried to calm the situation.

'Holt – we're in a war. We're all prisoners. Nobody's having it very good.'

'But some are having it better than others,' Holt retorted, almost eyeball to eyeball with the adjutant.

'Sit down, Mr Holt,' said Pett. 'You're going nowhere.'

Before Holt could reply, Shaid glided into the room.

'Good evening, Major Pett,' he said, all charm. 'Good evening gentlemen. It is nine o'clock, yes? You are ready?'

Without a word Holt slung the canvas bag he had filled over his shoulder and made for the door. With great trepidation at his own daring, but equally determined, Birdie followed him. Pett glared, but said nothing to demean his officers in front of Shaid. He would fix them when they got back. He had decided to put that damned Yankee Holt under arrest and keep him confined to his room for the next three months. Birdie would be severely disciplined too for listening to the fellow and forgetting his duty. First thing tomorrow, on the carpet in front of the colonel.

Shaid led them outside the fort and along the miserable street, chattering brightly. They were making for a house at the far end. They could hear wailing music coming from it before they got there.

'Holt – what are we going to do? I mean, how are we going to get rid of this little squirt?'

'Relax, Birdie. We'll play it off the cuff. Let's get a drink under our belts and take a look at the local poontang before we start making plans.'

In a large downstairs room they found half a dozen men sprawling on big cushions smoking pipes. The musician in the corner was a lad of no more than fifteen or sixteen. The fat proprietor of the house bustled up and bowed low in front of Shaid.

'Here we are, my friends,' said Shaid. 'Be at home, please. Upstairs there are women for you. Young and beautiful and ready to show you any delights you prefer. And boys too, if that is your liking.'

'I say!' Birdie exclaimed, appalled.

'But first,' Shaid went on, 'we will smoke a pipe of opium together. And then a little fine resinous wine – very cooling, I promise. And then another pipe.'

He saw Birdie's expression.

'The sensations of the flesh are pleasant,' he said, smiling at him. 'And they can also be the gateway to spiritual pleasure.'

The proprietor was tugging gently at Shaid's sleeve, trying to lead him away for a private word. Perhaps he was worried about having two enemy officers in his establishment, or perhaps he merely wanted to arrange the price in advance. Whatever it was, he took Shaid into an inner room, giving the two officers a chance to make plans.

'Ever smoked opium?' Birdie asked, grinning.

'No. And I'm not starting now. We've got the picture, Birdie – here's what we do. We'll sit a while with him and pretend to smoke opium – only make sure you don't inhale the stuff. After a time we'll say we want to go upstairs for a screw. My guess is that Shaid will stay down here and smoke himself insensible.'

'How are we going to get into the compound without him?'

'We'll sneak out after he passes out and go in under the wire again.'

'Right. It might be tricky getting back to our billet without him. We're supposed to be accompanied at all times, you know.'

'I'm not going back to the billet, Birdie.'

'You must be mad! What are you going to do – run for it?'

'I'm staying with the men. The guards will never notice one more in the compound. I'll go with them when they're moved on.'

'But why?'

'Two reasons. I'm not going back to have that bastard Pett kicking my tail in the morning. And somebody's got to help those men in the compound. You could come with me, you know.'

Birdie's face reflected his agony of indecision.

'I want to . . . I really do . . . but I've given my word to stay. So have you. Doesn't that mean anything to you?'

'Not a damned thing when there's work to be done. Anyway, I promised not to escape. I'm simply transferring myself from the officers' quarters to the enlisted men's quarters. That's not escaping.'

Birdie sighed.

'I can't do it, much as I'd like to.'

He looked shamefaced at his own lack of courage. Holt put his hand on his shoulder.

'That's OK, Birdie. I understand. You can be more use to me here anyway. When I go upstairs, keep that tick Shaid amused. Keep him down here smoking opium if you can. If not, then buy him what he wants upstairs while I slide off into the night. Got me?'

'Right,' said Birdie. 'I'll cover your withdrawal from the scene of the action. If it's boys the little bugger's after, I'll keep him supplied with them till he passes out.'

'Good man. Don't let on to anyone tomorrow where I've gone or they'll come and pull me out of the compound. Just say I've gone over the hill and they'll be searching the desert for days. They'll never think of looking in the prisoner compound.'

Shaid came back with the proprietor.

'My dear friends, I have been arranging matters. Can you give this man money for the entertainments?'

He was quite brazen about it now he had them here. Birdie winked and delved into his pocket.

'The party's on me, Shaid. Bring on the dancing girls.'

Cushions were placed for them on the floor and they sat round a bubble-pipe with a mouth-piece each.

'Breathe in very slowly and gently,' Shaid instructed. 'Savour the opium. It is grown in Turkey and is very best quality. Let it take possession of your soul. You will like it.'

They pretended to smoke, listening to Shaid's long tale of the boredom of being stationed in a small garrison town. He had once in his life visited Istanbul and he told them proudly about it and all he had done there.

After a time the proprietor brought them wine in an earthenware jug and poured it into little cups without handles. It was heavily resinated and tasted much like disinfectant.

They went through the bubble-pipe performance again. Shaid was getting very relaxed and was lying on his side, smoking dreamily. He had run out of conversation. Birdie prattled on about England and school and playing cricket. Holt wondered if the opium was getting to him. Time to make a move.

'I feel like going upstairs,' he announced.

'Go ahead, old boy,' said Birdie. 'Maybe we'll join you later but I want to tell Shaid about cross-country running first and the time I won the school cup.'

Shaid just waved a hand elegantly.

The proprietor took Holt's arm as he stood up. Holt pointed upwards and was led carefully up a flight of rickety stairs to a balcony running round the inside of a small court-yard. There were closed doors round the balcony. The proprietor muttered away, probably giving a sales talk on the qualities of his wares. He stopped at a door, called something through it and bowed Holt in.

Holt shut the door behind him and looked round. It was a small room with one square window in the wall opposite, which must open on to the outside of the building. Might be just what he needed.

The light of an oil lamp revealed a woman lying on a bed up against the wall to his left. He dumped his pack and went over to sit by her. There was no way of talking to her but he wanted to get her in a friendly mood so that she wouldn't start to scream if he exited through the window.

She was a plump woman, somewhere in her late twenties, he guessed, though it was hard to tell with these people. She had a lot of frizzy dark hair falling about her shoulders and she was wearing a long embroidered tunic.

Holt smiled at her, but her eyes gave little evidence of interest. He gave her a few piastres. That livened her up to the extent of taking his hand and pressing it to one of her big breasts.

'OK,' said Holt, making his voice as friendly as he could. 'You're all paid for downstairs and that was a present for you. I've got to hang around here in case my little chum Shaid gets suspicious. So as it's been a hell of a long time since I got laid, let's see what you can do.'

He stripped off his clothes and joined her on the bed.

'Your turn,' he said, tugging at her tunic. 'Show me what you're hiding under your night-shirt.'

She sat up to haul it over her head and lay back again naked.

'Well, you're a whole lot beefier than I like my women, if I had a choice. But you've got all the regular equipment, kid,' he said, patting her fat belly.

She cooed at him in her own language and stuck her chest out at him.

'They're big, all right. You're built like a football tackle. Ever tried weight-lifting?' he asked, running his hands over her warm flesh.

It was good to be touching a woman again. Holt realised how badly he had missed it since he had been taken prisoner. Unattractive she might be, and this was a hell of a time to be

61

fooling around with a whore. But he needed it.

He ran his hand up the soft inside of her chubby thigh and she obligingly parted her legs for him.

'What's a nice girl like you doing in a place like this?' he joked.

The woman ran her finger-nails down his spine and he stopped talking and let his body take over. She knew her trade and Holt had been frustrated for far too long. Their encounter was fierce and brief.

Afterwards, Holt gave her a cigarette and lit one himself.

'Great, kid,' he said, smiling at her. 'And the hell of it is that I don't know whether Birdie paid for all night or just one time. And I guess you can't tell me.'

She chattered at him while he lay thinking about his next move. There was a light tap on the door.

'I say, Holt – are you there?'

'What is it, Birdie?'

'Our little friend's gone into one of the rooms up here to amuse himself and I'm being shown into the room next to you. The coast's clear below.'

'Thanks, Birdie.'

'Good luck, old boy.'

Holt got up and dressed while the woman looked at him curiously.

'Look, kid, it's not that I don't think you're tops or anything like that. It was great while it lasted, but you know what these sudden romances are like. I've got to go.'

She stretched out on the bed, pushing her breasts up with her hands into impressive mountains of flesh. Her legs were parted in invitation.

Holt grinned at her and gave her a few more piastres.

'If I weren't in a hurry I'd give you another belt. But duty calls. So long.'

He took his bundle and left the room. There was nobody about on the balcony. In the room below he found two or three men half-asleep over their opium. The proprietor was there as Holt made casually for the street door.

'Thanks for the ride. You'll never get the Good Housekeeping Seal of Approval for this place but I guess that won't bother you.'

The fat man bowed, not understanding a word, and murmured something that probably meant come again soon.

In the street, Holt waited in the shadows for a moment or two to make sure there were no guards about. Then he set off for the prisoner compound.

Chapter 7

The prisoners were moved on the next day. Holt, curled up asleep on the ground, was wakened with the others by the Askars striding into the compound at first light, cracking their whips and shouting '*Yellah, yellah*!'

The men pulled themselves to their feet, groaning or grumbling, and filed out of the compound gate. Holt stayed in the middle of them, not wanting to be noticed.

Not all the prisoners left the compound. Three or four lay where they were, even with the Askars thrashing at them, either dead or too far gone to be able to stand. They were left behind for the Arab guards to dispose of.

That day Holt learned the hard way what the march was like. Up front, Raghib Chaoush rode his skinny horse at a walk, five or six paces ahead of the column, never hurrying, never dawdling, just a steady plod.

The leaders of the column, Holt noted, were Sergeant Parks and a man with corporal's stripes on the tattered remains of his shirt. The rest of the column was strung out over a hundred yards, no cohesion, no rhythm, just a long string of men walking in the same direction. Half-way along the column two Askars rode on mules, one on either side. There were two more at the rear to whip on the stragglers.

At the beginning of the day's march the British soldiers clung together in little groups and the Indian soldiers did the same, but after a couple of hours, there were no more groups. Each man was struggling to keep going blindly oblivious of all the others.

Holt let himself fall back to the rear of the column to see what it was like there. The weakest and most ill of the men were at the rear, British and Indian together. One man was hobbling along bare-foot with a terrible limp. Another was staggering with his mouth open, eyes blank and face blurred with pain. There was an Indian, gaunt to the point of emaciation, muttering prayers incessantly under his breath.

Holt fell in step alongside a small British soldier with a thin face, pale under his tan.

'What's your name?' he asked.

'Sharp, sir. B Company, Second Battalion.'

'Why does everyone walk separately? Wouldn't it make it easier if you talked to each other?'

'There ain't much to talk about, is there?'

'The Turk in charge – what's he like?'

'Raghib Chaoush, that's his name. Never says a word to anybody, sir.'

'I've no marks of rank on me. How did you know I was an officer?'

Sharp grinned feebly.

'I can smell an officer a mile off.'

'Can you? I thought the officer smell had worn off me by now.'

'Begging your pardon, sir, only an officer would ask such questions.'

They marched on in silence, feeling the heat as the sun climbed higher and higher into the cloudless sky.

Holt's presence had not gone unnoticed. Sergeant Parks had spotted him in the column right off and mentioned it to Corporal Dunsden.

'Officer in the ranks? You sure, Sarge?'

'Positive. You saw him yourself in the compound back there when Captain Vince-Halliday came down and started the punch-up with the guards. He was with Vince-Halliday and that chinless wonder Partridge. I saw him belt a couple of guards before they jumped him.'

'You're right,' Dunsden agreed. 'It's the same one. He talks funny.'

'I think he's an American or something.'

'More fool him to be with us.'

'Use your head,' said Parks. 'He's joined the column because he wants to. He's got something in mind. He could be
back in Mosul with the other officers if he wanted to, sitting
on his arse and eating three meals a day till the war ends.'

'You're right, Sarge. See that bag over his shoulder – what
do you reckon he's got in it. Map? Or even a gun. What do
you think he's up to?'

'How do I know?'

'If he made a run for it on his own from Mosul, they'd
pick him up in no time,' Corporal Dunsden speculated. 'This
way with us he's camouflaged till the right chance comes up.
He's escaping, all right, mark my words.'

'Like where to?' Parks asked.

Dunsden had no answer to that but persisted with the
thought.

'He's got to be on the run or what's he joined the march
for, you tell me that. He's waiting his chance. And I wouldn't
mind going along with him.'

At midday, when the sun stood at its highest and fiercest
point in the sky, Raghib pulled his horse to a stop and dismounted without a word. The men at the front end of the
column sank gratefully to the ground near an outcrop of
rock. The men were strung out over two or three hundred
yards by now, despite the efforts of the rear-guard Askars,
and Holt was having to help one of them to stay on his feet.

They reached the stopping place and the man collapsed
silently on to the ground. Holt handed him his water bottle
and the man gulped greedily at it.

'Steady on – not too much at once!'

Before Holt could have a drink himself, the Askars began
to shout *'Yellah!'* To his amazement, Holt saw that Raghib
had remounted and the column was straggling on again,
though the last men had only just reached the stopping
point.

A man with corporal's stripes came over and held his hand
out to Holt.

'Corporal Dunsden, sir.'

Holt shook his hand briefly.

'These men at the rear have had no rest at all, Corporal.'

'You'd do better to march at the front with us, sir. At the back they're nearly all down with dysentery. You can catch it easy from them if you get close and it spreads like wildfire.'

Holt helped a couple of men to their feet and got them moving before the Askars' whips did it for him.

'Corporal, why don't you march as a unit instead of trailing along like this?'

'We're not a unit any more, sir. It's no use pretending. There's still a few of us in some sort of shape, but not many. You join our group, sir, and we'll look after you. We'll draw your rations for you tonight and show you how to cook it.'

Holt nodded. To get any sort of control over the column, he was going to need the support of the non-commissioned officers.

They plodded on through the blazing afternoon, some of the men becoming almost delirious in the heat. At dusk they came to a Turkish supply depot, a straggle of mud-walled buildings. The men lined up automatically as they arrived, sitting or lying on the ground. Holt watched as Sergeant Parks went into the ration building and came out with an Arab storekeeper.

The Arab walked along the line of men counting them, closely followed by Parks checking the count. He knew very well that the storekeeper would cheat on the number of rations to be issued if he was given half a chance.

At the end of the count there was a short and heated discussion between Parks and the Arab in Arabic, to Holt's surprise. The sergeant obviously had hidden talents. They seemed to reach some sort of agreement and went into the building.

Holt followed them in to see what was happening. The Arab was measuring out the rations of flour from a barrel into a sack held by Parks. He used a large metal mug to measure. One mug of flour per man per day.

Parks scowled briefly when he saw Holt watching him. The

thought crossed Holt's mind that the sergeant was well placed to organise a bigger ration for himself if he wanted to.

Parks took his sack to the head of the line and the men filed past him. To each one he ladled out a mug of flour. Some of the men just took it in their cupped hands, some collected it in a piece of cloth, one or two had flat round stones to use as plates. A group of four Sikhs had a tin biscuit box in which their four rations were put.

'Got your ration with ours, sir,' a private said to Holt. 'Come over here and we'll show you how to cook it.'

Holt followed him to a bit of bare ground where he met Privates Shalley and Bailey. Shalley had collected sticks for a small fire, while Bailey had filled their water bottles from the big tank where Raghib Chaoush was giving his horse a drink. Bailey mixed the flour with water and kneaded it into dough on a flat round stone. Corporal Dunsden was lying flat on the ground blowing the embers of the tiny fire into a blaze.

'What we do is make one big chapati from all our rations together and then cut it up between us.' Private Shalley explained. 'It seems to go further that way, sir.'

'That's the total ration, is it?' Holt asked.

'Yes, sir. One cupful of flour per man. Only sometimes we get given rice instead of flour and that's a bloody nuisance to cook.'

Shalley looked up from the fire.

'We pick up a few extras sometimes in this group, sir. We've not given up. We're just biding our time. Like you.'

There was a pause. Then Corporal Dunsden spoke.

'Have you got a plan, sir?'

'Well, it's about time somebody did something,' Holt answered, misunderstanding him.

'You're absolutely right, sir,' said Dunsden. 'High bloody time.'

'First of all,' said Holt. 'I think I'd like to address the whole company.'

The others looked at each other in surprise. They had not expected that.

'Dunno about that,' said Shalley. 'Most of them will be asleep as soon as they've eaten – and Christ knows it don't take long to eat what they give us to live on.'

'Don't you think it would be wiser just to keep it among ourselves?' Dunsden suggested. 'They can't all escape, you know.'

'Escape?'

'You're planning to escape, aren't you?' Dunsden asked.

'There's no way of escaping from here,' Holt told him. 'Where to, man? The whole country is a prison. There's nowhere to hide, nothing to eat and every native is after your hide. You think you're badly off here – believe me, Corporal, it's better to be a prisoner of the Turkish army than a prisoner of the Arabs. I've tried both and I know.'

'So what are you here for, eh?' Dunsden asked.

'How many men were in your column when you started, Corporal?'

'When we left Baghdad there were two hundred men. Why?'

'The ration count tonight was a hundred and twelve,' said Shalley.

'So what's happened to the others?' Holt asked.

'They've fallen out, sir,' Dunsden answered, puzzled at what the officer might be getting at.

'What do you mean by fallen out, Corporal?'

'He means they're dead,' Shalley offered.

Dunsden flushed.

'That's the way it is,' he said. 'And what do you reckon the ration count will be by this time next week, sir?'

'We may have got to our destination by then,' said Holt.

'What destination's that? We thought you had a plan.'

'Certainly, Corporal. My plan is to stop this shocking waste of life.'

'How can you do that?'

'For a start we can start rattling that Raghib Chaoush at the head of the column. He needs taking down a peg or two. Give me a shout when supper's ready. I want a word with Sergeant Parks over there.'

69

While he had been talking to Dunsden and his men he had noticed that the sergeant had lit a tiny fire of dry sticks by himself in a corner near the supply building. As Holt approached, he saw Parks crack two eggs on to a piece of smoke-blackened tin over his fire.

The sergeant must have some sort of deal going with the storekeeper, Holt thought. Either he paid for the extra food, if he still had any money, which seemed very unlikely, or he took a bribe of food for letting the storekeeper undercount the men's rations. To Holt that was a very serious offence.

'Saw you talking with the lads,' said Parks casually. 'Are you going to do a bunk with them?'

He smiled up at Holt, a hard and sardonic grin.

'You're the senior soldier?' Holt asked, not smiling in the least.

'That's right, sir. But don't let it bother you. It don't mean much here.'

'Well, you're superseded now, Sergeant. I am the senior officer in charge now and you're going to help me make sure that every one of the men left gets to wherever we're going.'

Parks chuckled.

'Excuse me, sir. An old sweat told me when I first joined up that you should always laugh at officers' jokes even if they're not funny. If I was you, I'd concentrate on helping yourself.'

Holt ignored the insolence and stared pointedly at the eggs frying on the tin.

'Your ration seems extra large to me, Sergeant.'

'I'm a growing lad, sir.'

'How did you get it all?' Holt asked sharply.

'I'm good at card tricks. And that's the truth.'

'I see. I'll ask you to explain that to me later. At the moment I want to speak to the men before they fall asleep.'

He'd have to get to the bottom of this ration business as soon as possible, he decided. And if he found that Parks was cheating the men, he'd take his stripes away and promote Dunsden to sergeant.

70

He made his way to the line of men propped up against the mud wall of the building. At the end he stopped and looked. Fifty yards away, off by himself, Raghib Chaoush was sitting on the ground by his tethered horse. A very solitary man, that one, thought Holt.

This might be a good moment to make contact with him. But as Holt walked towards the seated figure, an Askar got up from the ground where he had been squatting on his haunches and barred the way.

'It's all right,' said Holt. 'I want to speak to your sergeant.'

He pointed to Raghib. The Askar unslung his rifle from his shoulder and pointed it at Holt's belly.

'Very well. If he's busy right now I'll leave it until to-morrow,' said Holt, extricating himself from the situation, though he knew perfectly well that the Askars spoke not one word of English.

He walked back and positioned himself half-way along the straggle of prisoners slumped by the wall and set his canvas bag on the ground.

'Listen to me,' he called out briskly. 'My name is Holt. Lieutenant Holt. I'm here to help you. I don't know the ropes yet or what your main problems are, so you must tell me.'

'Try walking for a month on an empty stomach,' said a voice from the line.

'Yes, that's one thing I've got to take care of. I want any of you men who have complaints to bring them to me.'

That raised a feeble laugh.

'Good, I've amused you. We could use a few laughs around here. Now, first thing – I've brought some bandages and oil. There's not a lot, so just take what you need and no more. Particularly those with burst blisters and foot sores.'

One or two of the men got up and moved over to inspect the contents of the bag.

'Right, carry on,' said Holt. 'I'll talk to you again tomorrow when I know a bit more about what's going on.'

He'd made contact with the men. They knew he was with

them and would look to him to do something about their plight, he thought. So he felt he ought to make a start with Sergeant Parks and the rations.

Parks had long since finished eating and was sitting by his tiny fire with one of the Indian soldiers. To Holt's considerable surprise, the two of them were playing chess with a pocket set. Parks had already taken a good many of his opponent's pieces.

'You play chess, sir?' he asked, looking up.

'No. I want to tell you, Sergeant, that you can be replaced as senior noncom if it becomes necessary. And I can always appoint someone else to collect the men's rations.'

'As I'm the only one who can speak a bit of the lingo round here, that would be a bit silly, sir. The storekeeper would rob us blind. They're all on the fiddle, the Arabs – you've got to watch them like a hawk and play them at their own game.'

'As you can speak their language, come and explain to the guard that I wish to speak to Raghib Chaoush. He won't let me through.'

Parks took his opponent's queen before answering.

'That Turk's not much of a talker. Be a waste of time.'

'Is he a bully?'

'I don't know what *you'd* call a bully. He orders the Askars to use their whips on anybody that falls behind in the march.'

'I think they do that in their own army, so maybe that doesn't count.'

'He's what you might call an educated Turk,' said Parks. 'As I heard it, he was apprenticed to the English telephone company in Constantinople when he was a lad. Speaks very good English, for a foreigner. Joined the army when the war started and they sent him to sort out the Armenians. Turks and Armenians don't seem to get on together. The Turks slaughtered thousands of them – whole villages, men, women and children. Don't ask me why. Raghib didn't have the guts for it. He came out of it half off his rocker. He goes out on his own every night to sleep because most nights he wakes up screaming his head off.'

The Indian soldier had made a fatal move after losing his queen. Parks made his own final move on the board and said 'Mate.'

'Is what you've told me true?' Holt asked.

'Hard to tell. Turks are such liars. But it's as good a story as any to explain why he screams in the night.'

'OK, Sergeant,' said Holt thoughtfully.

'I'll tell you something else, sir – they've eaten your ration over there.'

Holt swung round and marched across to the fire where Dunsden's group sat.

'My ration ready?'

There was a silence.

'It's been taken,' said Private Shalley.

'Taken? Who took it?'

'We cooked it for you,' Corporal Dunsden protested. 'You can't expect us to guard it as well.'

'Very well,' said Holt, revising his views about Dunsden. 'Corporal – in the morning before we move off you will parade the sick men separately. There's a pencil and some paper in my bag. Make a list of the names of the sick men and what is wrong with them. That's an order.'

Chapter 8

At first light Sergeant Raghib saddled his horse and led it to the water tank. While it drank he cupped his hands and washed his unshaven face. Something caught his eye by the supply building and he turned to look.

The prisoners were lined up in columns of three, sitting on the ground. For the first time since they had been handed over to him at Baghdad to take north, they looked something like a company of soldiers instead of a beaten rabble. Raghib did not like the change.

To add to his surprise, he saw at the back of the depot one of the prisoners he couldn't remember seeing before standing with the storekeeper and another Arab. The prisoner counted out money into the Arab's hand and took by the mane a donkey that he held. The donkey stood fast until the storekeeper gave it a quick kick, then it ambled along with the prisoner.

Raghib watched open-mouthed as the man with the donkey came round the front of the depot to where the prisoners were lined up. He saw the one he knew to be the British sergeant salute the other as if he were an officer. He heard the sergeant report:

'Forty-six British troops, twenty-eight Hindu Indians, forty-two Moslem Indians – on parade, sir! How much did you pay for that moke?'

'How many sick, Sergeant?' Holt asked.

'All of them.'

'I know that. I mean too sick to last the day's march. Get Corporal Dunsden over here at the double.'

'Yes, sir,' said Parks sarcastically. 'And what the hell shall I do if he won't come? Cancel his leave?'

Holt was standing for no nonsense. He shouted:

'Corporal Dunsden!'

Dunsden got up from his place in the ranks and sauntered over to Holt. 'Corporal, last night I told you to prepare a sick list. Where is it?'

Dunsden reacted belligerently.

'What the hell does it matter whether ten men have got dysentery or fifteen or twenty? We've got no medicine and we can't do anything about it. I've got burst blisters on my feet – I'm unfit to march. So bloody what? Everybody's got blisters. One man's got an open wound in his belly the size of a plate.'

'Who?' Holt demanded. 'What's his name?'

'I don't know what his bloody name is!'

'Then go and find out and put it on that list.'

'What for?' Dunsden practically screamed at him. 'What good's a list going to do?'

'At least they know that somebody cares what happens to them,' Holt answered calmly. 'The more we are treated like cattle, the more we must conduct ourselves like human beings. Otherwise we shall be cattle.'

'It's all right for you to talk – you've been on this march one day. We've been on it for weeks.'

Holt took a pace forward to address the ranks.

'Men – today nobody is going to fall out. We're all going to see to that. We're a unit and we've got to stick together and help each other. If we don't, we've had it and they've won.'

'We've lost already,' said Dunsden.

'No, we may have lost a battle at Kut but we haven't lost the war yet and we're not going to lose it. Get that into your head, Corporal.'

Dunsden was almost hysterical as he ranted:

'Don't bloody preach to me! I fought a long campaign

75

with these men, all the way up from the Gulf to bloody near Baghdad. And after that we stood a five-month siege at Kut till we were starved out. None of us have had a decent meal for nine months – look at us, bloody skin and bones! When this march started I carried men on my back if they couldn't walk – and every one of them died. Don't start telling me about sticking together now!'

Raghib had seen enough to confirm his suspicions. The prisoner he had not seen before was obviously an officer and intended to take charge. He must have slipped into the column back at Fort Mosul. He must be taught a lesson at once.

Raghib shouted an order to the waiting Askars and Holt's address to the men was drowned by the cracking of whips and the shouted 'Yellah!' as the column was herded out.

Holt was furious at being interrupted.

'Tell the men to stand fast,' he ordered Parks, and then at the top of his voice he shouted 'Raghib Chaoush!' to attract the Turk's attention and get him to hold the Askars for a moment.

Raghib turned away, mounted his horse and rode slowly from the depot. Holt doubled over as a whip slashed across his back in a blaze of pain. Parks pushed him quickly into the column before the whip could fall again and Holt stumbled along with the others, his brief authority humbled by simple brutality.

The worst casualty among the sick was Private Sifton. Parks lifted him on to the donkey Holt had bought and got it going. Sifton collapsed forward so that his head rested against the animal's neck and his feet trailed along the ground. But at least he hadn't been left abandoned for the Arabs to finish off.

When Holt had recovered from his pain and had his anger under control he made his way forward to the head of the column until he reached Raghib Chaoush and kept pace beside his stringy horse.

'Sergeant Raghib, I shall ask you to delay the start of the march in future until my parade is over.'

There was not the slightest indication that the Turk had even heard him. He sat hunched in his saddle, staring blankly forward.

Holt tried again.

'Between Samarra and Mosul alone you lost thirty-one men from this column – did you know that?'

Still Raghib took not the slightest notice.

'Sergeant Raghib, my name is Lieutenant Holt and I want to work with you to ensure that everything is done to check this stupid waste of lives. That would be to the advantage of both of us. For a start, it would help us if we knew how far it is to our eventual destination.'

Raghib turned his impassive face to stare at Holt.

'As an officer you should not be with us,' he said slowly. 'You were not with us before Mosul or I would have seen you. As you have chosen to be with us, you are no more than the others.'

'A life is a life,' said Holt. 'We do not wish to waste them.'

Raghib spat into the sand at Holt's feet.

'What worth is there in saving a life that is already worthless?' he asked.

'Sergeant – even if you have given up hope yourself, why should we?' Holt asked. 'It is your duty and your responsibility to treat us honourably.'

'Is it I or is it this dried-up and forgotten wasteland that treats you badly?' said Raghib.

'It's your country,' Holt reminded him.

'And you have invaded it and lost. Now you must pay the price. Go back into the column before I call an Askar to whip you back.'

'We shall speak again,' said Holt firmly. But the threat made him halt while Raghib's horse plodded on and the head of the column caught up with him. He was reasonably satisfied. He had opened what he intended to be a continuing dialogue with the Turkish sergeant. For now that would have to be enough. Another opportunity would come later.

In the furnace of midday they came to the well Raghib was making for. It had a low wall of dry stones round its edge, otherwise it would never have been found.

Raghib dismounted and looked down the well shaft. Then he picked up a piece of stone and dropped it in. He listened as it bounced off one side to the other, until it hit the bottom with a flinty crack. The well had run dry.

The front end of the column arrived and the men took in the situation. Dismayed, they sat down on the dusty ground, while Raghib took out his field-glasses and surveyed the horizon towards which they were travelling.

Gradually the whole of the column straggled up, learned the truth and flopped down. The Askars collected in a group apart from the prisoners and drank from the water bottles hanging at their saddles. The prisoners eyed them in pure naked hatred as they guzzled their water.

Holt stood at the dry well, looking over the men and speculating on how many were going to fall out that afternoon. He saw Parks drinking from a water bottle he had kept hidden in the bundle of kit he carried slung round his back.

Parks saw his look.

'I warned you – you've got to look after yourself round here,' he said.

Dunsden came towards him, grinning stupidly.

'You feeling thirsty, Lieutenant Holt, sir?'

'I've been thirsty before, Corporal.'

'Look at them,' said Dunsden, waving around. 'Bloody crows' meat. How many are going to make the next lap, you reckon? Can you smell something? That's the smell of death hovering round us.'

'I've seen action,' Holt said tersely.

'That's different. That's the smell of battle. This is a tired and stale smell.'

Holt walked away from him and over to where Raghib was taking a swig from his water bottle.

'Sergeant Raghib, when is the next water?'

Raghib ignored him.

'Where are we going?' Holt insisted.

Raghib hung his bottle on his saddle horn and mounted his horse.

'Along the northwest supply route,' he said. 'To the next ration depot.'

'Is that where we stay?'

'Tonight. Tomorrow we move on.'

The first glimmering of information, Holt thought with some satisfaction.

The Askars were yelling and the prisoners were hoisting themselves to their feet. Holt hurried over when he saw three men prostrate on the ground and an Askar using his whip on them viciously. One of the men got himself to his hands and knees, then pulled himself to his feet and staggered after the column. The two others lay where they were, not even wincing as the lash fell on them.

Holt knelt by the nearest one and tried to get him up. The Askar cut at him twice expertly, once across the bare arm and once across the back. Sick with pain, Holt stumbled after the column, muttering to himself 'I'll get you for that, you bastard, if it's the last thing I do.'

Two men had been left behind. Maybe they were dead already. If not, the sun would kill them before the day was over, if wandering Arabs didn't find them first and slit their throats.

Corporal Dunsden fell into step beside Holt and steadied him with an arm round his shoulders.

'You really ought to give up this leadership lark, sir. It don't help you or us.'

'We'll see about that,' said Holt, straightening his stinging back.

With no water at midday, the men were straggling badly after another hour. Holt picked out a soldier who looked fitter than most – one he had spoken to before.

'You're Private Sharp.'

'That's right, sir.'

'Good. If you'll help me with the stragglers, Sharp, I'll pay you. There'll be lots of stuff you can buy at the next depot if you have money. Food or a water bottle – whatever you need.'

'I can't help you, sir. Keep your money.'

79

'Well then, let's just help one of them between the two of us.'

'It's better if they die, sir,' said Sharp. 'They've got the dysentery. As long as they're alive and with us they're spreading it. They're better off dead.'

'No, they're not. There will be a depot or a town up ahead. When we get there I shall try to buy a cart and a mule. Then they can travel without marching and they'll be isolated from the rest of the column.'

But Private Sharp shook his head and kept on walking.

By the time the column reached a village in late afternoon, Holt's simmering anger at the lack of response from the men boiled over and led him into real trouble.

It was the usual sort of collection of mud hovels with ragged natives looking half-starved themselves and ready to cut a throat for a handful of rice. But as the column went down the one street that led right through the village and out the other side, Holt noticed a Turkish officer lolling in an open doorway.

The men slumped to the ground as Raghib dismounted. They were too exhausted to think of food or water yet, but that would come in a while. Holt took Sergeant Parks by the arm and led him to the building where he had seen the Turk in uniform watching the column come in.

Three Arabs with rifles had been posted outside the door now that the prisoners were in the village. Holt pushed past them and into the shabby earth-floored room the Turk used as office and living-quarters.

Holt was very angry indeed. He wanted something done about the men suffering from dysentery.

The Turkish officer glared at the two prisoners who had forced their way into his private quarters. He had no way of knowing that Holt was an officer, nor would he have cared anyway. Prisoners were prisoners, cattle to be herded along with a bare minimum of precious water and food to keep them alive.

He started to shout at Holt and Parks.

'Sergeant Parks, tell him you are only the interpreter acting on my orders,' Holt instructed.

Parks spoke in Arabic to the Turk, disclaiming responsibility for what his superior officer was making him do.

'Right,' said Holt. 'Now he understands that, tell him I have come to insist that something is done immediately about our sick. I want no excuses from him – I want action and I want it now.'

'I'd be a bit careful if I was you,' Parks advised. 'They're like little tin gods, these officers. Let me reason with him a bit and offer him a few piastres if he can do anything for us.'

Holt was too wound up to listen to common sense.

'Just tell him what I say!' he shouted at Parks.

Parks began to speak, his face blank. Before he got to the end of his first sentence, the Turk began to talk in a threatening manner. As Parks continued, the Turk moved closer to Holt until they were face to face.

Parks fell silent as the Turk harangued Holt.

'Don't waste your breath,' Holt barked at him. 'I don't understand a word you say. And I don't damned well care. We had twenty men with dysentery this morning and by tomorrow we'll probably have another twenty. These are men for whose welfare you are responsible. I expect you to do something about it.'

The Turk reached out and put his hand over Holt's mouth to indicate that he should shut up. Infuriated, Holt grabbed his wrist and pulled the hand away violently.

'You won't shut me up that easily!'

The Turk lost his temper and barked an order to the guards. Two of them moved in fast, grabbed Holt's arms and twisted them up painfully behind his back. They marched him out of the office, with Parks and the other guard following.

When they took him round the back of the building, Holt thought they had been ordered to shoot him. Then one of the guards holding him kicked his legs from under him and when he fell, put a foot on his throat to hold him still. The other guard pulled Holt's boots off.

Parks touched the third guard on the arm and spoke to him. The Arab shrugged him away. Parks gave him money trying to buy Holt off. The guard took the money and waved Parks away. When the sergeant tried to reason with him, the Arab shoved him away hard and prodded him with his rifle until he got the message and took himself off round the corner.

The other guards had immobilised Holt by putting his ankles between the sling of a rifle and its barrel and twisting it tight. One of them held the muzzle, the other the butt, and they hoisted his legs into the air. The third guard came up, swishing his whip.

Sick with fear, Holt realised at last that he was about to be bastinadoed. The guard with the whip raised his arm and thrashed him across the bare soles of his feet. Holt clenched his teeth, but could not stop himself from crying out loud at the searing pain.

The guard had given him four agonising strokes and was just warming to his work of crippling Holt when a shouted order stopped him. Through a haze of pain, Holt saw Raghib Chaoush approach. He spoke sharply to the Arabs and they released Holt.

Holt sat up, wincing with pain, and put his hands on the burning soles of his feet.

'Put your boots on,' Raghib said, not even looking at Holt.

'I don't know if I can. Why did you stop them from carrying out their orders?'

'There is no need to punish you with the whip. The march will punish you enough. When you move on tomorrow your feet will be swollen and painful. You will suffer badly. If you cannot march, you will be left behind to die.'

He walked away and Holt eased his boots on to his throbbing feet. An unknown and minor Turkish officer had given him a lesson in how utterly helpless he was.

Chapter 9

By morning Holt's feet were very painful and he dreaded the march to come. He hobbled along to where the men were being issued with a large bun of black bread each. Corporal Dunsden came up to him.

'See what this leadership lark gets you.'

'Never mind that, Corporal. We have to get water bottles for the men who haven't got one. I've still got some money. Get Sergeant Parks to go with you and buy as many bottles as we need. Or something to carry water in.'

'To hell with that,' said Dunsden. 'I'm scarpering.'

Holt looked at him, not understanding the word.

'I've had enough,' said Dunsden. 'Understand? I'm going to make a run for it. There's transport over there.'

Holt looked in the direction Dunsden had flicked his head briefly. Raghib's lean horse stood unattended, saddled up and with a water bottle and bedroll behind the saddle.

'Don't be a bloody fool, Dunsden! They'll shoot you down.'

'They've got to catch me first and that's the only horse here. I've checked. I reckon it can out-run the mules.'

Before Holt could say anything else, Dunsden sauntered away, making towards the horse and trying to appear casual. When he got close to it, he made a rush, grabbed the reins and swung himself up into the saddle. The horse pranced and reared once as Dunsden kicked it with his heels and then took off at a gallop.

The prisoners cheered as they saw the corporal making his break. The Askars rushed on to the scene and loosed off their rifles at him, but he was well away.

The Askars and local Arabs stood shouting at each other until Raghib came out of the door of the Turkish officer's billet. He listened to them, gave a short order and went back inside. The Askars herded the prisoners back into line to draw their ration, as if nothing had happened.

Parks came up to Holt shaking his head.

'Bloody silly thing to do. Why didn't you stop him?'

'I couldn't,' said Holt. 'By the time I realised what he was up to, he was away.'

'I don't like the look of it, sir. These natives aren't worried. It's as if they know he can't get far and so they don't have to bother.'

'My own thoughts too, Sergeant.'

'How's your feet? Have you rubbed oil into them?'

'Yes, I'm all right.'

When the column started its day's march, Raghib was mounted on a bony mule. The Askars cracked their whips and shouted their eternal '*Yellah*' and the men moved along the narrow street to the outskirts of the settlement. After the last mud hovels there was a flat space with a dusty tree or two before the track started again across the scrubby land.

There were twenty or thirty Arabs in the open space, jabbering around something. Raghib walked his mule into the crowd and the prisoners followed him blindly. The Arabs moved aside and fell silent.

Corporal Dunsden's body hung upside down and naked from one of the trees. They had tied a rope round his ankles after stripping him and hoisted him up over a branch until his dangling arms were a foot or two off the ground. There was a big blood stain on the dry earth beneath him where his throat had been slashed. Two boys in rags were throwing stones at the swaying body.

Holt stared in disbelief.

'Look at that!' said Parks thickly. 'They've cut his balls off as well. They're worse than bloody animals.'

Raghib issued orders to his Askars, who unslung their rifles and moved in on the crowd. The Arabs shrank away, back towards the village. Raghib sat where he was on his mule, staring in front of him.

After a while the prisoners sat down where they were, waiting to be moved on when Raghib was ready. They all kept their eyes away from the body on the tree.

It didn't take very long. They heard shouting and wailing, then an Askar returned leading Raghib's horse. Another prodded two men along with his rifle. They had both been roughly treated and were bleeding about the face and mouth. One of them was carrying the horse's saddle-bag and holding his other hand to his mouth, where an Askar's rifle butt had knocked his teeth out.

They stopped in front of Raghib. He said something to an Askar, who knelt in the dust to check the contents of the bag. Holt saw him pull out Raghib's few possessions – a razor, soap, several clips of ammunition and some dried dates. When Raghib was satisfied that nothing had been taken, he nodded and the Askar repacked the bag and put it on the horse.

Raghib got off the mule and on to his horse. Holt went forward quickly.

'Sergeant Raghib, that man is a British soldier,' he said, pointing to the tree. 'We can't leave him there.'

Raghib nudged his horse forward as if he had not heard. Holt clung to his stirrup.

'That man is a corpse,' Raghib said. 'You can do nothing for him.'

'We can bury him at least. You must wait.'

Raghib stopped his horse and turned in his saddle to shout orders to the Askars. Then he rode on. The whips cracked and the column trudged after him, but no one stopped Holt as he walked back to the dangling body.

The little crowd had returned to see what happened to the men who had stolen the horse and saddle-bag. But Raghib had done nothing to them, only retrieved his possessions.

As Holt went close to the tree and saw how Dunsden had

been treated, he began to shake. The corporal had clearly been badly beaten and stoned before he was killed.

He couldn't reach the rope knotted round Dunsden's ankles. He would need a knife to cut him down. He looked round as if to ask for one and saw the silent Arabs crowding in on him. Then he was really afraid.

The tail end of the column with its Askar whipper-in was moving away in the distance. Holt realised that unless he got out quick, he'd be dangling alongside Dunsden inside five minutes, stripped, beaten and mutilated, waiting for his throat to be cut.

He turned away from the tree and walked briskly towards the column. 'No panic', he told himself. The first stone hit him just above the kidneys. He broke into a hobbling run, his beaten feet on fire. The stones came showering after him and he was hit several times more before he reached the sanctuary of the column.

That day's march was agony for him. His feet were so swollen that his boots were torture. He dare not take them off or he would never get them back on and would be compelled to march barefoot, which would be even worse.

But that night, racked with pain in body and mind, he tackled Raghib once more.

They stayed that night at a small ration depot. When they had eaten and the men were asleep on the ground, Holt limped slowly towards the single fire forty yards away where he knew the Turk was.

He was about ten paces from the fire when Raghib's voice said:

'Stop there.'

Holt stood still and looked at the Turk sitting on the ground by his fire with a blanket round his shoulders.

'Do you understand the word barbaric?' Holt asked. 'It means like wild animals, not like human beings. The murder of Corporal Dunsden this morning was barbaric.'

'He was an enemy,' said Raghib with indifference.

'He was a prisoner of war.'

'He was running away.'

'Then it was your duty to catch him but not to let him be butchered. There are rules, even in war.'

'How little you understand,' said Raghib. 'The people of that village are starving. They wanted my horse to eat. The Turkish army has taken all their crops and they have nothing. When you starve and you see your children starve, there are no rules. I wonder if you will keep your rules when you are starving.'

'Yes, I shall,' said Holt. 'I am a man, not an animal.'

'Well, you didn't bury your friend,' Raghib observed with a sneer.

There was no point in answering. Raghib knew very well why Holt could not bury Dunsden.

'A question,' said Holt. 'Why did you stop them when they were beating me on your officer's orders?'

'I have already told you.'

'About the march punishing me? It was more than that though. My belief is that you are an honourable man under your toughness, Sergeant Raghib.'

'Go away now. I want to sleep.'

And so did Holt. He was all in, partly from the physical exertion of the long day's march and partly from the emotional shock of Dunsden's death at the hands of the Arabs. Despite his aching feet and the bruises where stones had hit him, he fell into the deep sleep of exhaustion.

The next day brought its horrors too. A few hours after the march began, before the usual short midday break, they came to the first stream they had seen along this desolate route.

It was a wide and shallow stream of clear running water, edged by shoals of polished pebbles and a single row of trees on each bank, nourished by the stream. To the dehydrated prisoners, living from mouthful to mouthful of stale water from storage tanks, it was a scene of incredible beauty.

The men at the front of the column saw the trees first and the glint of water in the sun. They broke into a shambling trot past Raghib's plodding horse to get to the stream.

Once there, they flung themselves full-length into the

shallow water, letting it soak through their rags and into their parched flesh.

Holt was right at the rear, supporting Private Sifton with an arm round his waist to keep him upright and moving. The donkey he had bought was carrying a man whose feet were open and festering sores and who couldn't even stand. Holt heard the cries ahead and looked up to see the line of trees.

'You're all right now,' he told Sifton. 'Another minute or two and you'll have all the water you can drink.'

As more and more of the prisoners came to the stream they jumped in and revelled in the cool water until it was packed with men. Arabs appeared on the far bank between the trees. They were from the village on that side and they had been alerted that something unusual was going on by the cries and shouts of joy as the prisoners rolled about in the water.

'Not far now,' Holt encouraged Sifton, who was only half conscious.

'We used to cycle through Epping Forest on the way to the sea at Southend when I was a lad,' Sifton babbled. 'Have you seen Epping Forest? Thousands of trees, tall as churches.'

He raised his drooping head and screwed his eyes up against the glare of the sun.

'Are there any trees here, mate?'

'Yes, there are palm trees near the water.'

The Arabs had decided that their stream was too precious for this ragtag mob of foreigners. Stones began to fly. They were jeering and shouting as they threw the sharp-edged rocks at the prisoners, forcing them back from the stream. Some of the men were holding their heads with blood trickling between their fingers as they retreated.

Gradually all the prisoners were forced away from the water by the bombardment. On the village side, a dozen boys rushed excitedly into the stream to shorten the range. They shouted with glee every time they scored a hit with a stone on the men opposite.

Three shots rang out and the Arabs were suddenly quiet.

The stone throwing ceased. Raghib Chaoush sat upright in his saddle on the bank, his revolver smoking in his hand. He had fired over the heads of the villagers as a warning.

The prisoners stared at him and gradually realised his intention. With a gasping cheer they rushed back into the water while Raghib kept watch on the villagers.

A few steps from the stream Sifton broke away from Holt and went tottering forward on his own. He fell into the water and lay drinking his fill. Holt dropped nearby into the swirling stream, feeling its coolness soak into his parched body.

Raghib left them for a little while to enjoy the sheer bliss of bathing in the stream. The Askars sat on their mules, waiting for his orders. The Arabs watched in silence from their bank, not understanding who these men in the water were, not pleased to see them, but perhaps aware that their need was too great to be denied.

Eventually Raghib gave the order and the Askars started their chant of 'Yellah! Yellah!'

The men emerged from the water and struggled into line without a murmur. Holt stood up, his soaked clothes plastered to his body. He felt good again.

But Sifton still lay face down in a back eddy of the water, floating aimlessly. Holt went to help him, but an Askar rode his mule between them and slashed at him with his whip. Parks grabbed Holt by the arm and pulled him out of harm's way.

'How long's it going to take you to learn?' Parks grumbled. 'You bloody well ask for trouble, you do. It won't do Sifton no good for you to get flogged.'

The Askar dismounted and waded out to grab Sifton by his shirt and turn him face up. Sifton's eyes and mouth were open and he was obviously dead, drowned in the stream. The Askar hauled him half on to the bank and began to strip him of his boots and clothes.

'Take this pebble, sir,' said Parks. 'Keep it in your mouth. It'll stop your throat closing up when you run out of water.'

Holt watched the Askar strip Sifton naked. He tried to pull away from Parks's grip.

'Mr Holt,' said the sergeant. 'Get it into your head – there's only two sorts of people on this march, the living and the dead. Sifton's dead. The living march up at the front of the column.'

'He was one of your men. Don't you care?'

'What difference does it make if I care or not? I've got problems of my own.'

Holt pulled loose from Parks and went to the bank as the Askar laden with Sifton's boots and clothes climbed out. Without a thought for the consequences, Holt grabbed him and flung him backwards into the stream. At the splash and shout, every eye turned to Holt.

The Askar came up spluttering with rage and rushed Holt, intending to knock him down and flog him senseless. Holt ducked the rush and landed a smashing straight right to the man's chin, knocking him out cold. There was a murmur of appreciation from the ranks.

Holt walked out into the stream and picked up the naked body of Sifton. As he brought it back to the bank, Raghib rode up to see what was going on. The Askar was sitting up, spitting and rubbing his jaw. Raghib said something to him sharply.

'This one I'm going to bury properly and not leave for the crows,' Holt told Raghib loudly. 'If you won't wait now, we'll bury him when we stop for the night.'

Raghib looked at him and said nothing.

Holt raised his voice even more so that all the column could hear him.

'If you'd helped him he might still be alive. He'll be heavier to carry now he's dead. We'll take it in turns.'

The men stared at him in amazement.

'He's off his rocker,' said Private Sharp.

'Shut your mouth,' Parks snarled at him.

When the column moved off, Holt went in the middle with Sifton's body slung over his shoulder in a fireman's lift. Pride kept him going for a quite a way but as the sun dried the cooling water out of his clothes and made him sweat, the going got harder and harder.

Sifton was little more than skin and bones – dysentery had wasted him away – but to Holt he seemed to weigh a ton after a couple of hours.

By mid-afternoon he was making very slow progress. The mounted Askar at the tail end of the column was getting nearer. It was the one Holt had laid out and there was an evil smirk on the man's face as he swished his whip and eyed Holt's back. His turn was coming and he looked forward to it.

Private Sharp, who had been told off by Parks, gradually edged up to Holt.

'Look, sir,' he said, sweat rolling down his face. 'What are you trying to prove?'

Holt looked at him through glazed eyes and didn't bother to answer.

Sharp pleaded with him.

'Don't try to shame us, sir. It don't mean anything any more.'

'I don't want you to feel ashamed,' said Holt. 'I want you to carry someone who can't walk.'

'He's not someone. There's no point. That's a bloody corpse you've got there.'

'All right, Private. If you see no point in carrying a dead man, then carry a living one. That man over there.'

The man Holt indicated was tottering along on rubbery legs, his eyes shut, at the end of his strength.

'I can't!' Sharp screamed at Holt.

Another ten paces and the man on shaking legs fell to his knees. His eyes opened in surprise and he stared vacantly ahead. Sharp stopped to look at him while Holt trudged on.

The rear Askar saw the man on his knees and shouted *Yellah!* swinging his whip round his head as he rode up. But the man was deaf to threats, past hearing and almost past feeling.

With tears streaming down his face, Sharp went back and heaved the man to his feet. And as he did so, one of the Indian soldiers took the man under the other arm and between them they got him moving again.

Chapter 10

It was nearly dusk when they came to the ration depot. Holt gave them ten minutes' rest and then organised a burial party. Parks stayed away, but Sharp and a few others volunteered to help.

They had nothing to dig a grave with and not the strength to dig it anyway. They found a suitable spot outside the depot and laid Sifton on it, his arms by his sides and covered him with rocks they collected until they had made a decent-sized mound. There was nothing they could make a cross or marker with.

There was no praying. Holt lined his volunteers around the mound and said simply:

'We lay here to rest Private Edward Sifton 927 of the Indian army. May he rest in peace.'

That was all. The men went off to draw their miserable rations and cook them. Holt went with them. No one talked about the death of Corporal Dunsden. No one wanted to think about it. In fact, no one talked much about anything.

Except Sergeant Parks. Holt was strolling up the depot street, trying to walk without limping, when Parks called to him.

'Mr Holt.'

Holt went over to where the sergeant squatted against the wall wearing a Turkish coat.

'You've got a greatcoat,' Holt observed without surprise.

'Well, you know how it is. The nights get a bit chilly. I've got something else. Look.'

He pulled down a lapel of the coat to show the head of a live chicken.

'You never cease to amaze me,' said Holt wearily.

'I'd like to talk to you, sir. Why don't you sit down.'

Holt did so, wondering what was coming next.

'This is a bigger depot than we've seen before,' said Parks. 'There's quite a lot of stuff here. I wondered if you'd care to come gambling with me tonight.'

'Surely you don't need my help, Sergeant.'

'Well, it's quite a procedure,' Parks explained. 'First I play cards till I've won some liquor. That's the easy bit. Then I pick the doziest-looking native and take him aside for a drink and while he's getting sloshed on my liquor, I tell his fortune. I tell him he's going to have seven wives and wind up a general in their army, because that's what they all want. Well, his tongue gets loose and he tells me all about his pals, like where they come from and their likes and dislikes. So then I go back and tell their fortunes, only this time I know enough about them to make them think I'm a wizard or something. And I charge them a coin or two for it. That means I've got some stake money, so we play the three card trick and they try to win their money back.'

Parks laid out three cards on the ground.

'There's the Queen. I move them about like this. Now, which one is she?'

Holt turned a card over.

'You're wrong, you see,' said Parks. 'I let them win some of their money back to start with before I go for a real killing when I've got them hooked.'

'Ingenious. Why do you want my help?'

'You've got money. You could stake me. I'll share half my winnings with you.'

'Can we buy oil and bandages here?'

'They've got everything here, sir.'

'I'll stake you then.'

'Right. I'll be in that building over there.'

As the men settled down for the night on the hard ground,

Holt made his round. The first two men he came to were shivering with cold in a corner.

'I'm making a list of everyone's names,' said Holt. 'It's time we had a nominal roll in this outfit. What's your name?'

'Private Hudson 443, sir.'

Holt wrote it on his piece of paper.

'OK, Hudson. What's your friend's name?'

'I don't know.'

The other man was staring blankly, as if he saw and heard nothing.

'Name and number?' Holt asked him.

'There's something wrong with his throat,' said Hudson. 'You can see how swollen it is. He hasn't said a word for days.'

'We'll have to give him a name then. We'll call him . . . what shall we call him, Hudson? Where were you born?'

'Me, sir? Stepney.'

'I'll put him down as Private Stepney then. Tell me about yourself, Hudson. Where's Stepney?'

'East End of London, sir, near the docks.'

'Were you a big family?'

He got no answer and tried again.

'How old were you when you joined up?'

'I don't want to think about it,' said Hudson slowly. 'Don't want to think about anything any more.'

'You're tired. I'll see if I can find you something to eat later on.'

'I was a boxer, you know.'

'A boxer?'

'I'll never do that again . . . I'll never even run again. I want to go to sleep and not wake up in the morning.'

'I'll bring you something to eat,' Holt promised, trying to cheer the man in the only practical way he could think of.

He continued on his round, his heart getting heavier as he listed names and saw how deep was the depression into which the men were plunged. Over half of them were ready to lay down and die now. The rest weren't all that far from it either.

He found Sergeant Parks in the ration depot building with an audience of about a dozen Arabs, mostly old men the Turkish army had no use for. There were a couple of women shrouded in tatty black with their faces covered. One of them had a swaddled-up baby with her.

The room was lit by two candles and an oil lamp. Parks sat behind an upturned chest with an Askar guard on either side of him.

The wily sergeant had his audience almost mesmerised as he felt the bumps on an elderly Arab's head and rambled on in Arabic about the man's character and fortune. Holt stood near the door and watched for a while before he spoke quietly.

'I've seen poles and canvas in the stores over there. We could make stretchers if we had them.'

'Bloody hell,' said Parks. 'I don't know if we can win enough to buy luxuries like that. This ain't the casino at Monte Carlo, you know. This bunch of natives don't own more than a few piastres between them.'

'Are we winning?' Holt asked, seeing Parks's well-thumbed and greasy playing cards lying on top of the chest with a few dates.

'It's not time to start winning yet.'

The Arab whose fortune had just been told pulled Parks's shirt open and kissed a large birthmark on his chest.

Parks grinned at Holt.

'That's my strawberry mark. This lot think it's the sign of the chosen of Allah. If only my poor old mother knew!'

He picked up his three cards and went into his spiel, getting members of his little audience to bet on finding the queen. Some were allowed to win. A thought struck Holt.

'When you've taken all their money, Sergeant, what stops them from just knocking you on the head and taking it back again?'

'That's why I bring the Askars with me. Mutt and Jeff I call them. They get fifty per cent of the winnings to make sure I don't get rolled after I've won.'

'I can see that protection costs as much here as it does

back in Chicago,' said Holt with a grin.

'Can you put a few more coins on the table?' Parks asked. 'Money draws money.'

Holt put three coins on the chest and took the dates for Private Hudson.

'I'll buy these off you, OK?'

As Parks carried on with his three card trick, letting some win and some lose, he said casually:

'One of this lot was talking earlier on about a railway. I think I got it right.'

Holt looked at him in sudden excitement.

'Where? Did he say how far?'

'He was pretty vague. They all are. Well, they measure in days' journeys, not miles.'

'Had he seen the railway or only heard about it from someone else?'

'He said he'd seen it.'

Parks picked up his cards and shook his head at the crowd. He'd just lost the last three bets in a row and was pretending that he'd had enough. But there was still money in front of him on the chest. As he pretended to scoop it up, the Arabs jabbered at him to make him go on. They'd been making easy money and they wanted more.

'All right, my beauties,' said Parks. 'As you force me to play on, I'll oblige.'

He winked at Holt.

'Time to start winning?' said Holt. 'I'll leave you to it then. They'll be bolder if they see you on your own. See you later, Sergeant.'

He drifted out of the building, going nowhere in particular. He wasn't ready to sleep yet and wanted to know how much Parks would win off the Arabs.

He sat for a while near a broken old cart at the end of the street. A muffled groan roused him from his thoughts. He got up and peered round the end of the building, just as the groan swelled up into a scream.

In the moonlight he saw Raghib, wrapped in a blanket and thrashing about in the grip of a nightmare, struggling, waving his arms about and crying out in fear and revulsion.

Raghib's horse was tethered nearby. It backed away frightened, and tried to break loose. Holt went to it and calmed it down.

Meanwhile Raghib had woken himself up and was sitting up with sweat pouring down his face. Holt moved from the horse in case his action was misunderstood.

When he thought Raghib had a grip on himself, he moved forward so that he could be seen. He was betting that the Turk would not be too anxious to go back to sleep after a dream like that, whatever it was, and might just be in the mood to talk to somebody. Anybody.

'Sergeant Raghib, can I talk to you for a minute?' he asked.

Raghib grunted suspiciously and stared at him. Holt took it as an invitation and sat down on the ground, two or three paces away.

For ten minutes or so they talked almost as equals until Raghib's nature asserted itself again and he ordered Holt to go away. But the American was well pleased and went to find Parks. The sergeant had cleaned out the Arabs and was dividing the loot with the Askars.

'Time to go shopping,' he said to Holt. 'I reckon you can buy quite a lot with your share, if that's what you want to do. The storekeeper will give you anything you ask for to get his money back. I'm going to treat myself to a square meal.'

By first light Holt had three or four volunteers making two stretchers out of poles and canvas, and others bandaging the feet of those in the worst way. He bought bread and eggs and gave them to the ones who needed it most, including Hudson and his friend Stepney.

Parks was finishing a hearty breakfast when Holt approached him with his piece of paper.

'I've made a list of all the men, Sergeant. Here it is. We'll have a roll call this morning.'

When Parks nodded, Holt continued:

'Something else. I want you to help with carrying the stretchers when we move out.'

That made Parks blink.

'Did you ask Raghib Chaoush about the railway?' he asked, ignoring the suggestion.

'Yes. The Germans started to build a railway out of Constantinople a year or two ago. I'm not sure when but I think it was before the war started. The idea is to cut right across this desert.'

'How far have they got?'

It was Holt's turn to ignore the question.

'If you help with the stretchers, Sergeant, all the men will help. They know you don't back losers.'

Parks said nothing.

'We'll parade in five minutes,' said Holt. 'And I want the roll calling properly. OK?'

'OK, sir,' said Parks thoughtfully.

He stood up and used his parade ground voice to line the men in columns of three, sitting on the dusty earth, ready to move out. Reading from Holt's list he called the roll and each man answered his name.

At the end of it he turned to Holt, stood to attention, and saluted.

'Eighty-three men on parade, sir. Twenty-five of them classified sick.'

'Thank you, Sergeant. I'll address the parade now.'

'Sir.'

'Now listen to this,' Holt said to the sitting ranks. 'There is a railway ahead of us. A railway the Germans are building. That's why you have been marched all this way – to work on the railway. It's beyond those hills you can see on the sky-line. I want you to understand that from now on the ground will get steeper and more difficult because we shall be climbing up. But that won't bother us because we know where we're going and we know that we're nearly there.'

He paused to let the information sink in. He could see from the rows of intent faces that he certainly had their attention.

'This is a major ration depot,' he went on. 'And it's the last before we get where we're going. Today two extra Askars are joining us – you can see their handsome smiling faces over there with the ones who've been tickling us along so far. And two extra mules have been issued to the column to carry food for us until we get to the railway. Right?'

'How far, sir?' someone called out.

'Silence in the ranks,' Parks ordered, though he too was dying to know the answer.

'Now understand this,' said Holt. 'Starting today, the weaker men will not straggle at the back. They will be at the front end of the column and the stronger ones will bring up the rear. Got that? We've acquired two stretchers. We can't carry anybody all the time, but we can give the very sick a turn on the stretchers when they need it. Today nobody is going to fall out of the column and be left to die on his own. *Nobody*. The ones who can march best will help the ones who can't and we shall all get where we're going.'

He paused again and then told them what they wanted to know.

'It's four days' march, that's all. Four days and you're there. And you're all going to make it. You are very brave men and a very remarkable company. I'm proud to be your officer.'

Out of the corner of his eye he saw Raghib swinging his leg over his saddle and the Askars nudging their mules towards the men, whips at the ready. He wasn't going to have that.

'Right, Sergeant,' he said quickly. 'Carry on. Move them out.'

'On your feet, you dozy lot,' Parks roared, as if they were back on their own barracks square. 'Left turn. By the right – forward. Take your time from the stretcher bearers.'

By the time the astonished Askars had ridden up, the column was on the move and not a back felt the whip.

It took them all that day to reach the foot-hills. They did well now that they were taking orders from Holt. The stretcher bearers and the sick went in front, the stronger men brought up the rear, helping anyone who stumbled or fell. The rear-guard Askars had a frustrating day of it, with never a straggler to flog.

At midday they halted briefly by an abandoned village. All that was left were a few broken mud walls and a well. The men were resting on the ground, trying to get out of the sun under the shade of the walls, when three scruffy Arabs appeared from nowhere.

They sat down near the tired men and put a small clay plate on the ground. Two of them had flute-like whistles and the other a small drum. They began their peculiar wailing music. The men watched and listened, glad of any diversion.

Raghib walked over to where Holt was sitting on his own.

'Lieutenant Holt, your men were good on parade this morning,' he said.

Holt nodded.

'They have done a good march today.'

'Yes.'

Raghib looked around at the resting men with a hard eye.

'I say this so that you will understand. They are inspired by the example you make. And this can be dangerous.'

'It's my duty to look after them as best I can,' said Holt. 'I want as many as possible to reach our destination.'

Raghib was suspicious.

'If that is all that is in your mind, that is good. But if your example leads to other things and makes trouble for me, I shall shoot you first. Then they will be like cattle again and I shall have no trouble with them. You understand?'

Holt nodded but showed no reaction to the threat. After a moment Raghib walked towards his horse.

'Get the men on their feet, Sergeant,' Holt called to Parks.

The men were lining up before the Askars started their 'Yellah!'

Private Sharp put a piece of black bread on the musicians' begging plate. Then he jingled two coins in his hand and pointed to one of the home-made whistles. The Arab handed it to him and took the money. Sharp hurried into the column before the Askar on the flank could get to him.

He blew into the whistle and tried the effect of stopping the holes with his fingers. Sharp had been a regimental bandsman and knew his instruments. After a few tries he managed a whole scale on the whistle, made a couple of false starts and then launched into a recognisable *Tipperary*.

One or two of the men in the column grinned and began to sing as they plodded along.

'It's a long way to Tipperary,
It's a long way to go . . .'

'By God!' said Sergeant Parks. 'I never thought to hear that again.'

Chapter 11

The hills on the skyline grew nearer as the column plodded on. Ridges of peaks appeared behind them. And at last the ground began to slope upwards and they were moving up a track along a valley, away from the everlasting scrub-land. The going got harder and harder and the bone-tired men were lagging badly. Holt, sweat-stained and unshaven, saw that the pace needed to be slower if his men were going to make it.

Painfully he speeded up to catch Raghib riding up front. Sergeant Parks made the effort to catch up with the lieutenant, worried about what he might do. He was in time to hear Holt say as he trudged alongside the gaunt horse:

'I must talk to you, Sergeant Raghib.'

Raghib, hunched on his big saddle, ignored him.

Holt tried again.

'Sergeant – I insist on speaking to you.'

The Turk turned his sweating face slowly towards the lieutenant and eyed him stonily.

'You insist, do you? I think you are in no position to insist on anything,' he said, softly and dangerously.

Parks recognised the implicit warning in Raghib's voice and fell in beside Holt.

'Leave him alone, sir,' he murmured.

Holt shook his head angrily.

'You still haven't learned, have you?' said Parks. 'It's no use talking to him like a human being. He's a savage heathen bastard with no feelings. He's seen so many people die that it don't mean anything to him any more. The only person he's sorry for is himself. He's full of that.'

Raghib pulled up his horse with a fierce jerk on the reins and turned in his saddle to face Holt and Parks.

'What do either of you know about me?' he flared at them. 'What do you know about anything at all? You know nothing except your King's Regulations and a lot of other words which you think are important because they make everything right in your own conscience. What do I care about your conscience? You came here to fight a war in my country and because you've lost you think that it's a shame and a pity. But this is *my* country and it's being robbed and destroyed by the Germans for their own profit. Your country is untouched and safe. Your army goes out to fight your enemies on other men's land. I am a Turk and I don't even know what you and the Germans are fighting each other for.'

He broke off and kicked his horse forward again.

'What does any of it matter,' he muttered.

Holt seized the chance at once.

'It matters a great deal that we get medical attention for the sick when we reach a settlement. And we cannot go into the hills at this pace. The men are too weak.'

Raghib said nothing for a while as his horse clop-clopped on. Then he looked at Holt.

'You spoke of honour some days ago,' he said. 'Do you have this honour, Lieutenant?'

'Yes, I do.'

'Then I put you on your honour not to try to escape while you are looking for medical help for your men when we pass a settlement. I will tell my guards to let you go with your sergeant.'

Holt nodded and dropped back into the column.

'Bloody hell!' said Parks in admiration. 'That's a step in the right direction.'

Holt thought of something and called out after Raghib.

'Sergeant Raghib – I cannot give you my word of honour not to escape, because it is my duty to try. But you may be assured that my duty to these men is stronger than the need to escape.'

Raghib gave no sign that he had heard.

'You must be bleeding mad,' said Parks. 'Fancy saying a thing like that just when he's given in to you.'

'Thank you, Sergeant. I don't need your views.'

They slogged on, passing no settlements or other sign of life. And that night there was no depot, only the stony hillside to sleep on and a handful of flour from the pack-mules. The ridges closed in on them as they pressed on the next day and the going was even harder than before. Holt and Parks stationed themselves at the end of the column to spur on stragglers more kindly than the rear-guard Askar with his whip. Holt told Sharp to march up at the front of the column and play marching tunes on his reed whistle as often as he had the breath and energy to do so.

The Askars no longer bothered to ride out on the flanks. On the rock-strewn hillside there was nowhere for anyone to go except forwards along the winding track. Half of them trailed along behind Raghib and the rest rode at the rear of the column.

'Look here,' Parks said to Holt. 'You said we'd reach a town or something in four days. Who told you it was only four days?'

Holt didn't answer.

'Is it right?' Parks persisted. 'Four days?'

Holt glared at him.

'Use your head, Sergeant. It's no use telling tired men they're nearly there. That means nothing to them. You've got to give them a target to aim at. Four days is a target they can understand.'

'Yes, but is it true?'

They shuffled round a bend in the track after the column that was winding its way round a shoulder of hillside. And they all stopped dead in their tracks at what they saw.

Until now the real mountains had been hidden from them by the foot-hills. They saw now that they were still on the lowest slopes. Off in the distance, great gaunt peaks of rock towered skywards, defying them. The winding track they were on looped away before them and vanished into mist where it met the real slopes. The men's last dregs of will-power and perseverance drained away as they stared.

The sun vanished behind a cloud bank. The hills round them seemed suddenly dark and cold. The sweat dried on exhausted bodies and the men shivered.

Parks found his voice first.

'How can there be a railway up there?'

Even Holt was daunted for a moment.

'Look, sir, how many men do you think we can carry up there? Look at them peaks.'

Holt nodded and walked slowly forwards past the silent men to where Raghib was peering through field-glasses at the track ahead.

'Sergeant Raghib – where is the railway?' he asked.

Raghib put his field-glasses away in silence.

'We cannot carry our sick any further today,' Holt announced.

'They are supposed to be soldiers. They can march,' the Turk answered.

'They can't march,' said Holt, not arguing, just stating a plain fact.

'If you can't carry them and they can't march, they will be left here to die.'

'No,' said Holt. 'We don't do things that way in our army. We will stop now and have our rations. In the morning you must give us another ration each and then we will march.'

By way of reply Raghib shouted to the Askars. They unslung their rifles. The prisoners who had sunk wearily to the ground got slowly to their feet again, seeing the signs.

Holt shouted for everyone to hear.

'We are not going any further today.'

He turned his back on Raghib and walked back down the column. About half-way he sat down on a rock.

'Sit down everybody,' he ordered.

The men eyed the Askars. One or two sat down and the rest hesitated, not knowing what to do for the best. Sergeant

105

Parks sat down firmly and that settled it. All the men sat down.

In complete silence Raghib got down from his horse and walked over to Holt. Five steps away he stopped and drew his revolver. He let it hang loosely at his side as he spoke to Holt.

'Get up and march.'

'Tomorrow,' Holt answered through clenched teeth. 'Sit tight, everybody.'

Raghib considered for some moments while the Askars watched and stood ready. The Turk had no choice but to maintain discipline, whatever force it took. He stepped up close to Holt and put the muzzle of his revolver to the lieutenant's head. He held it there without saying anything.

Sergeant Parks got up, moved across to Holt and sat down again beside him. Holt looked surprised but kept silent.

'Look, matey,' Parks said to Raghib. 'You shoot his head off and that makes me senior man in charge of this bunch. And I'll give the same order to them to sit tight.'

Raghib looked from one face to the other. He had no doubt that they meant what they had said. But he couldn't back down.

'You choose to die for the sake of your men?' he asked.

'It's as good a reason as any,' Holt answered, wondering if he'd gone too far this time. But like Raghib, he couldn't back down now.

Raghib held the muzzle of his gun firm just above Holt's left ear. But before the battle of wills could be played out to its bloody end, a volley of rifle shots rang out from the hillside above. An Askar, intent on the clash between Raghib and Holt, screamed and went over backwards clutching at his chest.

Everyone dived for cover behind rocks and Raghib's horse bolted along the track. Another Askar was hit and went rolling and kicking down the hillside. Whoever was doing the shooting had the sense to pick off the armed men first.

Hidden behind the rocks on the hillside above the track, a dozen bandits were firing from three different positions.

106

Parks and Holt picked out the firing points and pointed them out to Raghib. An Askar showed himself over the top of his cover to fire up the hillside, was hit and folded over.

Raghib yelled to the remaining Askars to follow him and ran stooping low along the track and up the hill further along in an encircling movement. At once Holt, Parks and Shalley dashed out of their cover to scoop up the dead Askar's rifles. They poured rapid fire at the bandits' positions to keep them pinned down while Raghib and his men got round them.

After a while they heard shouts and another outbreak of shooting above and guessed that the Turk had hit the bandits from the flank.

'You come with me, Shalley,' Parks snapped. 'You keep firing at them, sir, to keep their heads down while we get round the other side of the bleeders.'

Going into action, the sergeant was a different man, Holt noticed. He changed his cover and kept up a steady fire against the rocks where he knew the bandits were, even though he couldn't see them.

Parks and Shalley scrambled up the rocky slope and came face to face with three men dressed in rags firing down at the column. They killed the three before a rifle came round to point at them.

All firing had stopped. Parks waited for a while and then led Shalley down to the track again.

Up above Raghib was inspecting the dead bandits. He stared in anguish at the body of a boy no more than twelve years old. The boy had been hit in the neck and was covered in bright blood. His rifle lay underneath him and in his broad leather belt there was a knife nearly a foot long.

Raghib holstered his revolver and stood in mute and gloomy thought while the Askars searched the bodies for anything of value.

Down on the track Parks and Shalley handed round the rifles and daggers they had taken from the bandits they had killed. Shalley was agog.

'All we've got to do now is kill those gorillas up on the hill,' he said to Holt.

'Then what?'

'Then we're free. We've got guns and food on the mules.'

'Free to do what?'

'We'll have a good rest and sleep and we'll move on first thing in the morning with full bellies. And we'll go the way *we* want to go.'

'Which way's that – forward the way we are being taken or back the way we've already come?'

Shalley was too excited to bother with details like that.

'We'll get a map. What the hell's it matter? We're free, ain't we?'

'No, the whole country's a prison,' said Holt.

'You've run out of fight,' said Shalley. 'Not me. I'm going to fight for my life.'

Holt sighed.

'And you'll have to go on fighting, Shalley. Not just marching, you'll be fighting for every scrap of food along the way. You'll need food for eighty men every day and you'll only get it by taking it from the natives.'

'Not eighty,' said Private Sharp, joining in. 'We're only taking the men in good shape to march and fight. That's nearer a dozen.'

'And who picks them?' Holt asked. 'You?'

'They pick themselves.'

'I see. The survival of the fittest.'

'That's right.'

'Then pick your men and get going fast before Raghib and his apes get back.'

'No hurry,' said Shalley, licking his lips. 'We've got business to settle with that bastard.'

'You don't understand,' Holt told him. 'Raghib Chaoush and his guards are our passport. Without them the natives will have our throats cut so fast that we'll never know what hit us.'

'If we don't kill them, they'll report the escape at the next stop and the whole bloody Turkish army will be out looking for us.'

Sergeant Parks had been thinking it out.

'You're stupid, Shalley,' he said. 'Everybody's going to be after you anyway. You'll get no sleep by day or night. There'll be no help and no let-up. You've got no idea of where you are or where to make for. There's enemies everywhere. There's Turks and Germans somewhere and bandits – and the whole bloody population of this god-forsaken country's on starvation rations. You saw what the natives did to Dunsden when they got him down. You've got six rifles and a dozen clips of ammo. That should get you through the first couple of days.'

Parks put down the rifle he was holding, making sure that all the men saw what he was doing.

'Tell you what,' he said. 'Suppose one of them Askars' mules over there had stopped a stray round in the fight? It would make a lovely stew. Well, who's to say it didn't get hit? Couldn't let it go to waste. Right then, let's get its throat slit and skinned and cut up. Very tasty, mule stew.'

'Stow that!' said Sharp. 'You're coming with us, Sarge. We need somebody who can speak their lingo.'

The listening men had been weighing up the arguments on both sides. They trusted Parks more than Shalley or Sharp. One by one they laid down the rifles and knives they held.

Parks glared at Sharp. The thin-faced soldier put his gun down. Only Shalley still held an Askar's rifle.

'Look, Private,' said Holt. 'You've come this far. Hold on a while longer. We must get there soon.'

'Get where?' Shalley demanded shrilly.

'The bleeding railway,' Sharp answered for Holt.

'If I thought you had any chance of getting out of this country, I'd be with you,' said Holt. 'We need somebody to reach the outside world and tell them what's being done to us. Three quarters of our column nearly have died since this march started. What's happened to the other twelve thousand

109

men who were captured at Kut? Have they been killed off the same way?'

'That's none of my business,' said Shalley.

'Yes, it is. We're all responsible for each other.'

'You're not responsible for *me*!'

'Shalley, listen to me. We are men who have been robbed of everything – strength, health, dignity, hope, discipline, comradeship. When everything has been taken away from you and you are left with nothing . . . '

'You've always got one thing!' Shalley interrupted, his voice choking with frustration at his hope of freedom fading. 'And I'll tell you what it is – it's your name on a bleeding roll of honour. *Better love hath no man than this*. We've always got that to look forward to, haven't we? So who am I laying my life down for? Who? Why? Well, take it from me, I'm bloody well not!'

He pointed round the silent circle of listeners as he spoke.

'Don't ask me to do anything for him, or him, or him – or any of them. I could have got away if you hadn't stopped me. I could have survived. I'd have killed the bloody lot of them, Turk, German or anybody else who got in the way.'

His eyes filled with tears of rage as he ranted on.

'One thing I promise you,' he shouted, jabbing his rifle towards Holt. 'I'll outlast you. You haven't got much longer to go. I'll outlast you if we have to crawl right across the bloody mountains and back across the desert. *I'll survive!* And I'll go back home after the war and write the bloody rolls of honour for the church monuments. I'll tell them how twelve thousand men were cheated out of their lives, inch by inch. And all for nothing. They can drape a bloody Union Jack round that!'

As he ran out of words, a shot rang out. Shalley spun round and fell, hit in the shoulder. He bounced off the rocks and lay limply on the ground.

Holt looked round quickly. Raghib and his remaining Askars were above them on the slope between two huge boulders. One of the Askars was lowering the rifle with which he had shot Shalley.

Raghib's face contorted with rage. He grabbed the Askar by the neck and slammed him hard against the rough boulder. A continuous roar came from the Turk's wide open mouth and all his pent-up fury seemed to flow out of his body and into his hands as he strangled the Askar.

The Askar's face turned purple and then slowly black. His eyes were bulging from his head as Holt scrambled up to them.

'Raghib – stop it! You're killing him!'

Raghib kept his brutal grip on the man's throat, squeezing the life out of him. He turned his face towards Holt, his mouth still open and emitting the mindless roar of a man who has stifled a scream for a long time and is now letting it out.

As Holt stared aghast, Raghib found words.

'I have slaughtered men whose names I never knew . . . men whose faces I never saw! In one village I killed three children . . . their mothers' nail-marks are still on my flesh. I have killed hundreds . . . I have killed many hundreds . . . '

'Then don't kill this one!' Holt yelled, trying to get through to him.

Raghib's voice fell to a mutter.

'I am a killer . . . what is your word . . . barbaric. I am a slaughterer, a murderer, a butcher . . . you see how well I know your language . . . how many words I know for the taking of life.'

His eyes closed and he released his grip on the Askar's throat. The man slid down the rock-face and lay motionless. Raghib turned away and stumbled down the hillside. Holt followed close behind.

'Sergeant Raghib, those people you killed . . . ?'

'The Germans wanted workers to help build the railway,' said Raghib. 'It was decided to push the Armenians across the desert to be their workers. But the Armenians didn't want to go and so we tried to make them.'

'You were under orders?' Holt asked.

'Orders! To slaughter women and children so that the men will obey?'

'It's over,' said Holt. 'Forget it or it will kill you.'

'Every night when I sleep I kill them over again. Last night, the night before, tonight, tomorrow, tonight.'

Holt tried to calm him.

'Ever since I have known you, you have shown compassion. You are not required to judge yourself or condemn yourself. You are not called upon to punish yourself.'

'But I cannot free myself,' said Raghib. 'I am a prisoner like you.'

'You will be free eventually,' said Holt. 'You will be forgiven.'

'Who can forgive me for what I have done? God? You?'

Holt could understand Raghib's plight. No one could absolve him ever from the guilt he felt. Only death would free him from it. But before Holt had time to think of any words of comfort, a distant sound jolted both of them out of these dark thoughts.

It was the hoot of a railway engine.

'By God Almighty!' Parks shouted. 'It's the Lieutenant's railway. He said it was four days, didn't he?'

The weary men found new strength. With the Askars trotting their mules behind, they fairly ran along the track to where it climbed up a ridge. The railway was just beyond. They had made it.

Chapter 12

Coming down from the ridge, the prisoners had time to see all that there was to see of the rail-head at Ras-el-Ain. There were a few rows of tents, a barbed wire compound and two or three ramshackle timber buildings.

Uninviting though it looked, they shuffled towards it almost cheerfully. At least their long march was at an end. There would be food and water and a chance to rest.

The railway line from the west ended just before a half-finished wooden bridge over a deep gulley. Beyond that it would run through a cutting in a steep hillside. Over on the rails, well away from the unfinished bridge, stood a silent locomotive of a type unfamiliar to the prisoners and two or three wagons and carriages.

Raghib led his little column down off the ridge and into the cutting through which the line would eventually run. Gangs of men were at work with picks and shovels, shifting earth and rocks. German soldiers patrolled in pairs, rifles slung over their shoulders, keeping a sharp eye on the labouring prisoners.

Two men helped Shalley along. His arm bound across his chest with blood-stained bandages. He was pale, but he was alive.

The men in the cutting paused in their work to stare at the column coming through. As they leaned on their shovels staring, their appearance did nothing to cheer up the column. They were all naked to the waist, burnt nearly black by the sun and gaunt-ribbed.

One of them called out:

'Is Harry Hunter with you?'

And another recognised Sergeant Parks and called out his name.

'Who's that, then?' Parks asked.

A human scarecrow stepped forward.

'Private Stockman, Sarge. You remember me.'

Dismay spread quickly along the column as they realised the plight of men working on the railway. These men they saw, almost unrecognisable now, were those who had been ahead of them on the march from Kut. These were the strong and fit ones who had survived the march.

The Askars cracked their whips to keep the column moving.

'How long you been here, Stockman?' Parks asked as he plodded along.

'Not long – week or ten days. There's only twelve of us left from my platoon, Sarge.'

'What's the grub like?' Parks called back over his shoulder.

'Bloody awful. One day's work, one day's ration. You get nothing if you're too weak to work.'

Following Raghib, they filed over the half-finished bridge and up to the compound. They were lined up while a German officer and a clerk counted them. No effort was made to list their names. For all practical purposes they had ceased to exist. They had become anonymous labourers, to be worked until they dropped. Whether any of them lived or died was of no importance whatsoever to the men who ran the camp.

Holt was separated from the rest as soon as Raghib reported. He was taken under guard to the tent of the officer in charge. Major Hausmann was a man in his thirties, wearing engineer's flashes on his uniform. He was sitting behind a trestle table littered with maps and drawings.

'So,' he said to Holt. 'You are an officer but you have got yourself mixed in with ordinary soldiers.'

His English was good, though guttural.

'That is so. I am an officer in the Royal Flying Corps.'

'Aeroplanes?'

114

'Yes.'

The German nodded thoughtfully.

'The mastery of the air is going to be very important one day soon. And aeroplanes are useful to me in my work too. Look at this.'

It was a photograph taken from the air. Holt studied it.

'I am an engineer. That was the first bridge I built, before I was in the army. It is beautiful, yes?'

'Very fine,' said Holt. 'Now Major, I wish to bring to your official attention a number of complaints on behalf of my men.'

The German chuckled.

'You shouldn't be here at all. An officer in a labour camp is not right. But the Turks are always getting things mixed up. They should have sent you with the other captured British officers. Let's have a drink. Orderly – bring the brandy.'

'About my complaints,' Holt began, but Hausmann cut him off with a roar.

'Complaints! Everybody's got complaints. It's no use telling me – I can do nothing about it. I've got complaints of my own, but no one listens to them.'

The orderly brought in a bottle of raki and two glasses. The Major filled them and handed one to Holt.

'Prosit! Listen, I am expected to lay two kilometres of railway track a month through this terrible country, across hills and ravines. Two kilometres a month, with second-rate equipment and a labour force of skeletons.'

'If you gave the men proper medical attention and rations you'd get on faster,' said Holt. 'If they were properly fed they'd easily beat your target every month.'

'There's nothing I can do about it. I don't decide the rations or the facilities. I just have orders to build the track with the men they send me.'

'In that case, this line can't be of any great importance.'

'It is an artery of the German Empire,' Hausmann declared. 'The first empire built on man's technical mastery of his environment. When this line is finished, it will link

Hamburg on the North Sea through Constantinople to the head of the Persian Gulf and then on to India. Then the German army will kick you out of India. Look at the map.'

He traced the line across the map with his finger for Holt to follow.

'You've got a long way to go yet,' said Holt.

'Ja, ja! But we shall do it. We will drive the line through these hills and down to the desert you have just crawled across and on to Baghdad. And along the line will come more engineers to build dams and canals and aqueducts. Understand? Mesopotamia was the birthplace of ancient civilisation – the original Garden of Eden. But the natives have turned it into a desert with their goats and sheep and stupid ways.'

In the outer tent Raghib was listening. He was standing in front of a table on which a clerk was working, listing the numbers of new prisoners and Askars to take on the ration strength. Raghib spun out his report of the march, accounting for the dead Askars, not that anyone cared about them. But he could hear quite well what the major was saying to Holt and it made him think.

'We will make it bloom again with our technical knowledge,' said Hausmann. 'It will become a land flowing with milk and honey, as the Bible says, instead of a wilderness of thorns and sand. The lazy Arabs must go, of course. They are less than human. *Untermensch*, we say in German. And the Turks must go – they are as useless as the Arabs. We shall replace them with Armenians from the north of the country. The Armenians are intelligent and hard-working. And they are Christians.'

'That's all very well,' said Holt. 'But what about the Turkish Empire. It's been around a long time. Don't the Turks get a say in what you're planning for a big slice of their territory?'

'Have another brandy, Lieutenant. You must not be naïve about the Turks. They are barbarians and they have to go. They are in our way. They are worse than useless. For example, we tried to get them to move the Armenians down into this area to work on the railway and then to go down

116

into the plain to start planting and irrigating it. And what happened? The Turks slaughtered half a million Armenians getting them to move. Half a million! Men, women and children. I ask you, what can you do with people like that? Like the Arabs, they are too primitive to be civilised, whatever you do. They have to go.'

In the outer tent Raghib finished his business abruptly and walked out. His deepest suspicions had been confirmed by what he had overheard.

Holt's men were put to work straight away on the back-breaking job of levelling ground and moving earth. Holt himself was left alone. As an officer he was not expected to work. He could wander at will around the camp. Major Hausmann had not even asked him for his parole not to try to escape – which meant there was nowhere to escape to and no point in trying.

Raghib too was free to wander about as he wished. His task was finished now that his prisoners were handed over. His arrival at Ras-el-Ain was notified by Hausmann to his base by means of the telegraph that ran alongside the finished track. Eventually orders would come for Raghib to report somewhere, after the Germans had notified the Turkish army. But that might be a very long time, since the Turkish army was not famous for the efficiency of its paperwork.

There was no one for Raghib to talk to in the camp, even if he had wished to. He avoided the Germans, who had no time for him anyway. He despised the Askars. He kept well away from the prisoners, who had no reason to love him. He had plenty of time for his own thoughts and nightmares.

He took to watching Holt secretly, without quite formulating in his mind the reason for doing so. But he knew Holt to be a leader and a man of courage. He alone therefore was worthy of Raghib's interest.

Each morning at the same time Holt left the camp and headed towards the working parties on the bridge and the cutting beyond. It was almost as if he were the commanding officer making his morning round of inspection.

One morning, concealed behind a big rock, Raghib overheard a short conversation that confirmed his opinion of Holt.

Sergeant Parks and a squad of men were down in the gully beneath the timber bridge. Parks was pretending to work, shovelling vaguely at the earth as he talked to Private Shalley. Shalley's arm was still in a sling and he couldn't work. He had elected himself water-carrier and went round the working squads all day with a bucket of water and a dipper. In return the men fed him collectively from their own miserable rations.

Holt marched up to Parks.

'Good morning, Sergeant,' Raghib heard him say. 'How are things going?'

'Everything under control, sir,' Parks answered briskly. Then in an undertone that Raghib only just caught, 'I've briefed the men on the plan, like you said. And I've booked a seat for you on the train when it leaves.'

Holt said nothing for a while, looking across at the train standing on the lines on the western side of the gulley.

Then he grinned.

'First-class sleeper, Sergeant?'

'There aren't any first-class compartments,' said Parks. 'Apart from that I've got most of the details worked out. I'm still looking for a driver.'

Suddenly Parks began to dig energetically and Shalley moved off with his bucket. Holt turned slowly to see a German guard approaching. The German saluted him. Holt returned the salute and moved off.

Later that day Raghib spotted Holt up near the train. Something stirred in the Turk's mind and he went quickly and stealthily in that direction himself.

Holt made his way along one side of the train, studying everything in detail without stopping to stare openly. He looked at the flat wagons used for bringing sleepers and steel track up to the rail-head. He looked at the passenger coaches. He looked at the couplings and the brakes.

Opposite the engine foot-plate he stopped for a moment and glanced casually over his shoulder in the direction of the camp to see where the nearest guard was.

He had his hand on the hand-rail and was just about to pull himself up on to the foot-plate when Raghib came round the front of the engine. Holt stepped away from the engine at once, looking nonchalant. Raghib glanced at the engine and then at Holt.

'Good afternoon, Sergeant,' said Holt.

Raghib moved closer and reached out to touch one of the big driving-wheels of the engine. His eyes narrowed as his fingers ran over the steel.

'We have arrived at the same conclusion, you and I, perhaps,' he said.

'Sorry,' said Holt. 'I don't follow you. What are you talking about?'

'This railway runs to Adana,' said Raghib, ignoring the question. 'It is about eighty kilometres.'

There was a pause as Holt evaluated the information.

'Adana is a port,' Raghib went on. 'On the sea. From there a man could go anywhere he liked.'

Holt studied Raghib's face carefully.

'Why are you telling me this?'

The answer surprised him.

'It is because I am a Turkish soldier and in these times a Turkish soldier must be a killer. But I cannot kill any more when they order me to. And like you I am a prisoner. My whole country is a prisoner. We have all been captured by those men,' and he waved briefly towards the German camp.

'And so like you, Lieutenant, I wish to escape.'

Holt tried not to let his surprise show too much.

'What about your Askars – do they feel the same way?'

'They are not mine. They are only mercenaries and kill for whoever pays them. They work for the Germans now, not me. Their job is to guard the camp at night.'

Holt made his mind up.

'Look here, Sergeant Raghib, I trust you. But I don't know if Sergeant Parks and the rest of my men will.'

Raghib looked down at the ground.

'Of course. I was forgetting that you would not go without

119

your men. You and I could do it alone, you know.'

He looked Holt in the face.

'Your men have no reason to trust me, Lieutenant. But you can talk to them. It will be much easier to get away from here with my help.'

'I can't make any promises,' said Holt. 'But I'll talk to them.'

Chapter 13

At Ras-el-Ain the day's work began at sun-up and went on without a break until sunset. Only when it became too dark to see properly did the guards march the prisoners back to the camp and issue their miserable rations.

The tired men set to in groups to cook their food over little fires. By the time they had eaten it they were ready to sleep and get what rest they could on the hard ground before the next day's back-breaking stint began. All but a few, that was.

While the human skeletons huddled round their fires against the impending night chill, one or two slipped cautiously out of the ring of light. They picked their way over broken ground to the meeting place. Parks was there first, spying carefully round to make sure there were no Germans or Askars about. When he was sure it was all clear, he whistled softly. In a second or two Privates Shalley and Sharp slid out of the darkness and crouched beside him. And then an Indian prisoner.

The meeting place was up beside the silent train, well away from the camp. Holt came quietly out of the dark to join them.

Parks spoke very softly.

'I've found our man, sir. This is Fasil Engineer. He got his name from his job in the army. He's a train driver.'

He looked up as another figure loomed up out of the darkness and gasped when he saw it was Raghib Chaoush.

'Trouble!' said Parks succinctly. 'What do we do now, sir?'

'It's all right,' said Holt. 'I asked him to come.'

'What the hell for? He'll shop us.'

'No, he wants to escape too. He doesn't like it here any more than we do.'

'Well, that's a turn-up for the book!'

Raghib spoke.

'It will be easier if I help you. This is my country. I know where we are and where we can go. I understand the way things are done here.'

Parks growled suspiciously.

'Sounds fishy to me. You marched us like bloody slaves across miles of nothing. You starved us and beat us. You're on the same side as the Germans – so why do you want to help us? It doesn't make sense. You'd be deserting. They'd shoot you for that.'

'If we're caught escaping, we'll all be shot,' said Raghib. 'You as well as me.'

'Shot? For trying to escape? That's not right.'

'They would do it as a warning to the others. You must understand this. If you try to escape, you are putting your life at risk. If you are captured – bang! So you need my help, I think.'

'You still haven't said why you want to escape.'

'I hate the Germans more than you do. To you they are just the enemy. You fight them, maybe you beat them, maybe they beat you. It is all part of your job as professional soldiers. For me it is different. They pretend to be the allies of Turkey, but they have become our masters. They have taken over our country. On their orders I have done terrible things. And they regard me as no more than a useful animal. When they are finished, they will dispose of me and all the others like me.'

He spoke with such conviction that even Parks was convinced.

'All right, matey. But what about those bloody Askars of yours. We're not giving them a free ride, not after what they done to us.'

'They are not mine. They obey the Germans. I do not care what happens to them.'

'The Germans have put the Askars on permanent night duty,' said Holt. 'So that their own men can do guard duty in the day.'

'That's very handy to know,' said Parks. 'It'll be a darned sight easier to get the balloon off the ground if the Germans are all tucked up asleep at the time. The Askars will be skiving off asleep anyway, even if they're on guard duty. Right Raghib, my old beauty, you're in.'

'Good,' said Holt, relieved that Parks had accepted the Turk. 'Can Fasil handle this sort of locomotive?'

'He reckons the engine hasn't been built yet which he couldn't drive. But there's a bloody great snag we didn't know about.'

'What's that?'

'Fasil says that the engine'll take at least an hour to get up steam and it'll make a hell of a racket doing it.'

'An hour? Is he sure?'

'No use arguing with the expert, sir.'

'That puts a different light on things. It's no use clobbering the guards quietly and sloping off to the train as we planned if the train can't move for an hour.'

Parks turned to Sharp.

'You – get up there on that hill and keep an eye out for visitors. We're going to have to talk about this for a bit and we don't want any Askars tripping over us in the dark.'

Sharp nodded and crawled quietly up the slope.

'Well, we knew we'd need a bit of a diversion to cover the move out,' said Holt. 'But it's going to be a hell of a big diversion to keep the Germans busy for an hour while Fasil gets steam up. Got any ideas?'

'We must attack the most important thing for them,' Raghib said at once.

'What's that, then?' Parks asked.

'The railway itself. The officer in charge is fanatical about it. If it is threatened in any way he will concentrate all his men on saving it.'

'You're right,' said Parks. 'Hit the railway. And as we need the train and the lines, that means the bridge. Any thoughts on how we can have a go at the bridge, sir?'

'Yes,' said Holt.

They talked long into the night, making the best plans they could and trying to foresee the contingencies. When they were satisfied that the plan was as good as they could make it, they slipped quietly back into the camp and huddled in their dirty blankets to get what sleep they could before the sun came up.

During the next day Parks, Shalley and Sharp secretly passed on the orders to the working gangs. While the men dug and shovelled earth, carried timbers and hauled rocks away, the ones assigned to specific tasks in the escape plan began to steal and hide away the things they were going to need. Some of it was easily found, being in constant use – crowbars, chains, ropes. Some of the things they had been instructed to get had to be located first and stolen – night lanterns, buckets, kerosene, knives. Some of the equipment was in the stores, some in the German field kitchen.

It was easier than Holt thought. The Germans relied on the impossibility of getting anywhere as the main deterrent to escape. In consequence, Ras-el-Ain was a minimum security camp. Major Hausmann had only one lieutenant and a dozen German troops to act as guards, and the Askars for night duty. By day the German soldiers were patrolling the work areas to keep the prisoners at their labours and so it was not difficult for a man to slide away and steal what he had been told.

In three days Parks was able to report to Holt that they had cached away all the equipment they needed.

'Good,' said Holt. 'No point in hanging about then. We'll leave tonight. Pass the word round, Sergeant.'

'Right. What about Raghib? Is he still going with us or shall I get somebody to tap him on the head after dark with a pick handle?'

'You'll do no such thing. I gave him my word. I'll warn him it's tonight.'

Chapter 14

They waited for two hours after the camp had fallen silent for the night, to be certain that the Germans were sleeping. Then a whispered order from Parks sent the squads moving silently off to their assigned tasks.

First to go were the look-out men. Four of them were spaced out right across the camp, lying flat on the ground, a long string connecting them. By tugging it they could signal danger or all-clear from one side of the camp to the other and alert any squad nearby.

Down by the bridge, four more men were silently lifting planks from a stack to get at the lengths of thick rope they had stolen and hidden beneath. They coiled the ropes round their bodies and moved quietly towards the train.

Parks had the knives that had been lifted from the kitchen. They had been honed on rocks to razor-edges. He issued them to men he had chosen for their nerve and sent them off on their task.

One of them was Private Shalley. He eased himself over the bare earth towards the stores, where an Askar sentry was posted at night. As he had expected, the Askar was asleep on the job.

Lazy bastard, Shalley thought, he ought to be court-martialled for being asleep on guard duty.

He inched his way up to the sleeping man, taking care not to make the slightest noise. What he had to do must be done very quickly and exactly. Holding his breath, he moved in close to the hunched figure with its back to the wooden stores hut. Then in double-quick time he grabbed the Askar by his greasy hair with his left hand and pulled his head up. Before the man could cry out, Shalley slashed hard across his exposed throat with his knife. The man kicked and gurgled. Shalley cut his throat again, all the way round, to make sure, feeling warm sticky blood gushing out over his hand.

One of the men on the look-out string heard a noise behind him. He craned over his shoulder to see what it was, pressing himself close to the ground. He heard shuffling feet and tugged three times on the string.

The next man along squeezed closer to the earth and passed the danger warning along. Action round the camp froze as hissed warnings sounded.

It was a man coming out of the German tents. The look-out saw him silhouetted against the sky and waited, hardly breathing. If the German went far in any direction he would trip over some squad or other in the dark. There was a sound of splashing as the soldier relieved himself. Then he yawned and went back into his tent. Everyone stayed still for a while, to give him time to go back to sleep. The all-clear was tugged on the string and the squads went to work again.

By the water tank Holt held a guarded night lantern while his group collected their concealed crowbars. In the middle of it a suddenly stifled scream froze them as another Askar was dealt with, slightly less expertly. But no alarm was raised. If any of the Germans had heard it, they had no doubt taken it to be a night-bird.

'Get a move on,' Holt whispered. 'We haven't got all night.'

The men followed him towards the train. Parks and his squad were by the engine, fixing ropes to various parts of it. Raghib was with them.

Holt looked at his watch anxiously.

'We're running late, Sergeant. It's all taking longer than we allowed for.'

'Don't remind me,' said Parks.

Raghib glanced up at the night sky. There was a great deal

to be done before dawn. He began to wonder if they would make it.

A clatter of morse stopped them in their tracks. Seconds later a lantern came on in the telegrapher's tent, not two hundred yards away. Holt gestured to everyone to lie flat and keep quiet.

'Christ, that's torn it,' Parks muttered.

Private Rees crawled towards the tent, ready to deal with the emergency. In his hand he held a length of iron pipe. He stayed just outside the circle of light from the lantern in the tent and waited. He could see on the tent side the silhouette of the telegrapher taking down the message that was coming through. He heard the clickety-clack of the German acknow-ledging the message, then saw him stand up and come out of the tent. He eased himself forward, pipe ready to smash the man's head in, but Sergeant Parks appeared on the ground beside him and touched his shoulder. Rees looked at him and Parks shook his head.

They watched the German head away towards the tent lines in the camp.

'Why'd you stop me, Sarge?'

'The officer down there might have heard the morse clatter and if he didn't get his message, he'd come looking for the reason why. Just wait.'

The wait until the camp commandant came back with the telegrapher was nerve-racking. Parks took his knife from his belt.

'Rees, if we have to, we'll do it very fast and very quiet. If I say go, jump in and bash that Gerry over the head before he makes a noise. I'll take care of the officer. Under-stand?'

Rees nodded.

They waited while the commandant exchanged messages over the telegraph wire with base. Then he got up and came out of the tent. Parks and Rees gathered themselves together, ready to jump if they had to. But Major Hausmann moved off towards his tent, grumbling under his breath, while the telegrapher turned off the lantern and climbed back into his cot.

'Stay here and keep an eye on him, Rees. If he gets up again, deal with him. Only don't make no noise.'

Parks crawled back to the engine, where Holt was looking at his watch again.

'Can't be helped,' Parks told him. 'We're ready now. Fall in, you lot.'

They had four ropes fixed to the engine and ten men to a rope. In silence they took up their positions. Holt and Raghib among them on the ropes.

Working with the utmost caution, one man uncoupled the engine from the rest of the train. Not a clink of metal was heard as he released the coupling links.

Lantern in hand, Parks faced the teams on the ropes and flashed the light for one second.

Like tug-of-war teams at a village fête back home, the men leaned back and put all their weight on the ropes. Their legs thrust against the ground and they heaved with all their strength. But the engine didn't move an inch. It was like trying to pull a mountain over.

Parks flashed his lantern again and they relaxed and sank to the ground, arms trembling and chests heaving from the strain. After a minute's rest, Parks whispered to the front man on each rope:

'Pass this along. If anybody trips, let go the rope and roll out of the way. Now this time, when I flash the light, count up to five, take the strain for a count of five and then heave. Give it all you've got.'

They tried again. Forty men rose from the ground, took the ropes and heaved their hearts out until the ropes were creaking.

Half-way along one rope, an exhausted and frustrated man started a wailing cry. At once, the man behind him let go of the rope and clapped a hand round his mouth. They both fell.

The heaving fizzled out and still the engine hadn't budged. Holt and Parks climbed up into the cab to join Fasil Engineer.

'It's impossible, Sergeant,' Holt said quietly. 'We haven't

got the muscle power to shift it. We'll have to get steam up here and risk it.'

'No, they'd be on to us like a shot.'

'But we can't move it.'

'Don't you believe it, sir. Go back and tell them we'd forgotten to take the brakes off, that's why they couldn't move it. They'll be able to now.'

'You mean that Fasil had the brakes on?' Holt asked furiously.

' 'Course not. But the men don't know that.'

Holt climbed down again. Parks followed him, bringing two more ropes with big metal hooks on the ends. He hooked them on to the spokes of the driving wheels on each side and redistributed his men so that all the ropes were taken up.

Parks went back into the cab. The men readied themselves, waited for the lantern flash, paused for a count of five, lay back into the ropes for a second count of five and then gave it all they'd got.

Over the laboured breathing, a metallic rasp indicated that the wheels were turning. Up on the footplate, Parks spoke openly to urge them on.

'Now!'

The engine was just moving. The men's feet inched backwards as they hauled the iron monster. Parks jumped down from the cab and trotted along the sweating teams, speaking just loudly enough for them to hear him.

'Come on, come on, come on – it's rolling! One foot back, next foot back. Keep it rolling now! Heave, heave – she'll be rolling on her own in a minute. This is our ticket home – put your back into it!'

The engine was rolling at a perceptible speed as the forty men kept at it. Only the faintest of creakings and metal clankings could be heard. But it was enough to disturb the German telegrapher. Rees heard him stir and grunt. Silently, Rees crawled up to the tent and raised the flap, took aim and smashed the man's head in with one blow of his iron pipe.

He pulled the wires out of the morse key and smashed the key itself.

The engine rolled silently past the telegrapher's tent and behind a spur of hillside into a cutting. The men let it roll to a stop, now that it was concealed from the camp by the spur and sat down panting on the ground.

'Well done,' said Holt. 'We made it.'

'Sure we made it,' said Parks. 'But look up there.'

Holt turned to peer at the eastern sky. The first faint gleam was beginning to show beyond the crest of the mountains.

'Right, let's get on with it,' Holt snapped. 'Our cover's running out fast.'

Parks glared at the dim figures of the men sitting round him.

'All right, you lazy, idle men. You know what you've got to do, so get on with it. Quietly!'

In twos and threes the men slipped away, back to their own sleeping quarters. Parks and Sharp made their way to the stores hut, while Holt headed for the German compound.

Fasil and Raghib stayed behind with the engine. They filled the fire box with wood and waited. Raghib went out beyond the spur and crouched between the rails, so that he could see the signal when it came and relay it to Fasil.

At the stores hut Parks and Sharp dragged round the back out of sight the Askar Shalley had killed earlier on. The door was not locked. They went in and helped themselves from the big drums of kerosene. With two bucketfuls each, they went quickly down into the gulley spanned by the wooden bridge. They soaked the wooden uprights in four places, stood well back and threw lighted matches. The flames went up with a loud roar and licked round the sun-dried timbers.

They trotted back to the stores for more kerosene and set fire to the stack of timber used for bridge building. The flames shot twenty feet into the air.

Raghib saw the distant flare and ran back to the engine. Fasil flung a bucket of kerosene into the fire box, soaking the wood, and Raghib threw in a match and slammed the fire box door as the flames shot up.

Down in the prisoner compound, Parks dashed towards his men, who were pretending to be asleep in their proper places.

130

'Fire!' he shouted. 'There's a fire!'

In the German lines, Holt ran towards Major Hausmann's tent, also shouting 'Fire!'

The trick now was to spread confusion and panic, to keep the Germans off balance and fully busy so that they would have no chance to notice that the engine was not standing with the rest of the train. As the startled and half-awake soldiers came out of their tents, pulling boots on, they found Holt shouting 'Fire, fire!' and pointing down to the bridge. Without pausing to size up the situation, Major Hausmann ran towards his bridge, shouting at his men to follow him.

Meanwhile, Parks was organising the prisoners noisily.

'Come on, you idle men – form a line and get buckets of water down to that fire. At the double! Move yourselves!'

With much shouting and rushing about, the prisoners gradually formed a line from the water carts down to the bridge. Parks stayed by the carts, ostensibly supervising the filling of the buckets, which were then handed along the long chain of men to be thrown on the blazing timbers. Major Hausmann and his lieutenant formed their own men into another bucket line, while Lieutenant Holt rushed up and down both lines yelling incomprehensible orders, adding to the disorder and panic.

Parks was bellowing orders continuously himself as he filled buckets and handed them to the end man of the chain:

'Come on, get your backs into it. Get them buckets moving down the line faster. We'll never hold the fire at this rate.'

With satisfaction Holt saw that the confusion was almost total. Hausmann was so concerned to save his bridge that he had not stopped for a second to wonder how the fire had started or what else was going on and why. Sooner or later he would, and then the fat would be in the fire.

Holt glanced briefly towards the distant spur that hid the engine and saw with alarm sparks flying up into the sky for a moment or two. Fasil and Raghib were overloading the fire box to get steam up fast and flames were roaring up the funnel. Fortunately all attention was on the burning bridge on the opposite side of the camp. And somehow that attention had to be kept focused in that direction for a long time yet.

'Sergeant Parks,' he shouted. 'Keep the water coming. Water, I said.'

'Right, sir,' Parks yelled back.

Leaving the bucket chain to carry on, he sloped away towards the stores, taking Shalley and Sharp with him. They filled two buckets each with kerosene and eased back to the water tanks, where they slipped their buckets to the end men, alternating with buckets of water.

'Keep it coming, Shalley,' Parks ordered. 'Only don't get spotted.'

Shalley went back to the stores for more kerosene, while Parks and Sharp followed the progress of the buckets they had infiltrated, shouting encouragement as they trotted alongside the sweating line.

At the end of the chain, Parks grabbed the first bucket of kerosene to reach the end man and hurled it at the edge of the fire, which spread rapidly.

'More water!' he bawled, grabbing the next bucket. 'Sharp – get back up there and give Shalley a hand.'

Holt stood near the burning bridge, watching events. He turned unobtrusively to look towards the train. In the first faint light of dawn he could see clearly the two passenger cars and the flat wagons. Before long one of the Germans must notice that the engine was missing and raise the alarm. Holt dashed back along the bucket line shouting orders, and when he was safely out of bridge range, fell silent and trotted towards the ridge behind which the engine was hidden.

Raghib had left Fasil to get on with raising steam while he made a raid on the armoury in the German quarters. He collected a machine-gun, several belts of ammunition, half a dozen rifles and clips, a handful of grenades and a box of explosives. The rest of the weapons he threw out into the rocks and scrub where they would be hard to find. Then staggering under his load, he headed back towards the engine.

In the stores, Sharp and Shalley had run into trouble. Two of the Askars came upon them as they were filling their buckets from the drums. The Askars started to unsling their rifles. At once Sharp flung a bucket of pungent kerosene into the nearest man's face. Shalley, remembering the whips on the march, snatched up a crowbar and doubled up the other Askar with a smashing swipe to the gut. Then, measuring the distance, he brought the crowbar down on the head of the whimpering man, braining him.

Sharp followed up his own attack. As the blinded Askar stood gasping and rubbing at his eyes, Sharp swung the empty bucket by the handle and knocked him cold. He fell and lay limp. Sharp gave him one more mighty bash on the head for luck with the bucket.

The two men grinned at each other and got on with the job of hauling kerosene out to the firefighters.

Back at the locomotive, Holt helped the panting Ràghib stack the weapons from the armoury handily in the cab.

'Are you ready yet, Fasil?' Holt asked, while Raghib loaded the rifles.

Fasil tapped the pressure gauge. The needle had moved about half-way round the dial.

The Indian shook his head.

'Not ready yet, Lieutenant sahib,' he said anxiously. 'Need twenty, thirty minutes.'

Holt grabbed an armful of wood from the tender and hurled it into the fire box. Raghib left his guns for a moment to hurl their last bucket of kerosene in after the wood. The resulting roar and burst of flame almost engulfed the cab and singed all three of them.

'We've run out of time,' said Holt. 'I'm going back to organise the withdrawal. We'll spin things out as long as we can, but it won't be long. Stand by to give us covering fire.'

He jumped down from the cab and trotted back to the scene of the fire. It was practically broad daylight. The fire at the bridge was dying down. When he reached the spot, he saw that it was not so much the efforts of the firefighters but that most of the timber of the bridge had burned away. The Germans would have to demolish the charred remains and start again from scratch. He looked around for Parks.

'Are we ready yet?' Parks asked.

'Nearly – but he needs a bit longer.'

'No can do. The fire's over and they'll rumble us any minute. It's got to be now or never.'

'Come on, then. We'll fire our last shot, Sergeant.'

They sped back along the bucket chain and parted at the water carts. Holt made for the train to give Raghib a hand when the shooting started. Parks branched off towards the stores.

'Outside, you two,' he ordered Sharp and Shalley, still busy filling buckets. 'Get back to the line and warn everybody to make a dash for the train when I give the signal.'

The two put their buckets down and left quickly. Parks looked briefly at the two dead Askars on the floor. He opened the taps of all the kerosene drums to let the contents pour out on to the ground and kicked over the buckets his men had filled. He stood outside the door of the building, struck a match and threw it. A sheet of flame went up with a huge roar, knocking Parks over. He picked himself up quickly and dashed back to the Germans with their water buckets.

'The stores!' he shouted. 'Quick – or the lot'll go up!'

Led by their despairing and bewildered officers, the German soldiers filled their buckets and ran towards the blazing hut. The British and Indian prisoners filled their buckets and trotted after them. Then on a shouted 'Run for it!' from Parks, they dropped their buckets and changed direction, running hard towards the train.

Holt was up on the foot-plate. It was broad daylight and he knew what was happening in the camp when he heard the roar of the stores hut going up in flames.

'Come on, Fasil. Get this thing rolling.'

The Indian shook his head doubtfully, looking at the pressure gauge, still not showing full steam. He pulled a lever. The engine grunted and panted and began to move slowly backwards.

Major Hausmann saw with amazement his prisoners haring away across the camp. A mass break-out? Unthinkable! Then he saw that the engine was not standing coupled to the rest of the train. Before he had time to think it out, the engine came backing slowly from behind the ridge. Everything fell into place.

He shouted orders to his men. They dropped their buckets and ran for their tents to get their rifles.

The prisoners, led by Parks, panted up to the passenger cars. Parks gave Raghib a hand in placing the machine-gun on its mount on top of the end car. Raghib opened the breach and Parks fed in the end of a belt of cartridges.

The engine was coming towards them with agonising slowness. The German troops were racing through the camp, rifles at the ready.

'Push the wagons towards the train,' Holt shouted, lending a hand.

The men put their shoulders to the wagons and heaved.

'Sharp – have you fixed the telegraph wire?' Parks called down from the machine-gun post.

'Doing it now, Sarge.'

Sharp had taken the end of the wire from the dead telegrapher's tent and tied it round the end buffer of the rear coach. He had to make sure he got this right, to stop the Germans telegraphing ahead to stop the train. He looked at his handiwork. When the train moved off, it should strip the wire from the insulators on the overhead poles for miles.

Slowly the engine rolled up to the coaches and clunked against them. Two men linked up the coupling and jumped clear. On the foot-plate Fasil put the engine into forward. The wheels spun on the rails, the engine puffed and wheezed, then the train began to move slowly forward.

The Germans were firing as they ran. Up on the machine-gun Raghib cut the leaders down with a quick burst while Parks fed the belt in expertly. The Germans dived for cover and kept on firing.

'Get aboard!' Holt bellowed. 'We're going.'

The prisoners swarmed up into the coaches as the train got up to walking speed and accelerated. Raghib sprayed round with the machine-gun to keep the Germans' heads down. Then the train puffed out of their sight round the spur and into the cutting. Major Hausmann barked orders and his men got up and ran for the two trucks parked beyond their tents.

'Let me have a go,' Parks said to Raghib. 'It's about time I shot a *HUN* or two.'

Raghib grunted and changed places with him. Parks took the hand grips of the gun and swivelled it left and right to get the feel of it.

The train was moving at a good lick now, clacking along the track. After the cutting, the ground opened out again into a featureless plain. Parks watched as the two trucks, loaded with soldiers, came after them. They were catching up, one on each side of the railway line and the men in the back of the trucks were firing over the top of the cabs, aiming at the machine-gunners.

Parks sighted along the barrel, took a chance on the range and fired a long burst at the nearest truck. He saw the windscreen shatter, then the truck veered sharply away to the left. He had hit the driver. The truck hit a big rock with its off-side wheel and turned over, raising a cloud of dust.

He took aim at the second truck.

'Just come a bit closer, you bastard, and I'll have you,' he muttered.

But the second driver was taking no chances. He was holding his distance, waiting for the riflemen on board to knock out the machine-gunners before he closed up.

Parks heard bullets whistle past uncomfortably close. He glanced over his shoulder towards the front of the train and grinned at what he saw.

'Fire,' Raghib urged him. 'Shoot them.'

'No need, old son. Just watch.'

The train rattled over a wooded bridge that spanned a narrow gorge. The driver of the German truck saw the danger too late, being intent on the chase. By the time he hit the brake pedal he was too close. The truck went sliding forward on locked wheels through the dust and sailed over the edge of the gorge. Parks and Raghib heard the crash as it hit the bottom.

'Nobody left to chase us,' Parks said to Raghib. 'We'd better report to the lieutenant.'

The men in the coaches leaned out of the windows to crane up and cheer as Parks and Raghib walked along the swaying tops to the engine. Holt was in the cab with Fasil, helping him stoke. Parks stood on the edge of the first coach and looked down at them.

'We did it!' he yelled at Holt. 'We bloody did it!'

Holt smiled and yelled back.

'Sergeant Parks, I'll see you get promoted for this.'

Parks jumped down into the wood-filled tender and came forward into the cab.

'Thank you, sir, but I've got all the stripes I want. I'll settle for twenty-eight days leave, if you can fix that.'

Chapter 15

Two hours chugging through the deserted countryside took them to a spot a few miles outside Adana. Raghib was in the engine cab with Holt and Fasil, while Parks was back in the coaches, checking the stolen weapons and making sure the best marksmen had them.

Raghib had been watching the landscape for some time.

'We must stop now,' he said.

Holt nodded and told Fasil to stop. The train slowed down and groaned to a halt.

'Everybody off, Sergeant,' Holt called to Parks, who had his head out of a window.

'Right, you happy bunch of soldiers. This is the terminus. Off the train quick.'

Raghib explained the lie of the land to Holt. He pointed to the south.

'The sea is just beyond that ridge, about five kilometres from here. And the port is there. From here it will not take an hour if you march quickly. Maybe the Germans will be there expecting you.'

'In that case, we'll have a fight on our hands,' said Holt.

'Perhaps. But there will be other things to take their attention,' the Turk went on. 'What you call a diversion. Goodbye, Lieutenant.'

Parks had joined them and was listening curiously.

'You don't have to do this, you know,' Holt said to Raghib.

'We cannot leave the train here. It is too obvious. And a

diversion will make it easier for you.'

Parks butted in.

'Look, old son, don't think we don't appreciate what you've done. If I was you I'd just fade away into the landscape and lie low 'til things blow over.'

Raghib smiled.

'I know you would. But I must do things my way.'

Parks slapped him on the shoulder in a friendly manner and turned to his waiting men.

'Get fell in, you lot. And shake it up.'

The men assembled in lines of three. Holt shook Raghib's hand. There was a lot he wanted to say but he had no words for it. Nor had Raghib.

'Straighten that rank,' Parks thundered in parade ground style. 'Have you forgotten all the army ever taught you while you was in that little holiday resort back there?'

Holt looked at his tattered sergeant and scarecrow ranks. They had forgotten they were soldiers until he had reminded them and given them a common purpose and a framework of discipline. They were soldiers again now and they would fight if they had to.

'Move them out, Sergeant.'

Parks saluted, hatless though he was.

'Squad will move to the right in threes, right . . . turn! By the left . . . quick march! Get a hold of the step, you dozy men. Ep, ai, ep, ai, ep, ai.'

As the little column moved off, Raghib pulled the lever that started the engine rolling forward. Holt gave him a wave but the Turk was staring ahead and didn't see it. Holt trotted after his men to overtake them and get in front. A good officer led from in front. That's what they had taught him at Military Academy and that's where he intended to be.

He heard the train chuffing away behind him as it gathered speed. He did not look back at it. Raghib had his own war to fight and nobody could help him.

Worrying away in Holt's mind was the question of whether the Germans at Ras-el-Ain had been able to report their escape. If so, the port was sure to be heavily guarded. He ran over it in his mind. Both trucks had been smashed up and there was no other transport in the camp except for Raghib's horse and the Askars' mules. And they were all a lot slower than the train. The real danger was that the Germans had been able to repair the telegraph line.

Sharp had done a fair job of putting it out of action but the wire he had attached to the rear coach had broken after a few hundred yards and the rest of the line was there for the Germans to use. The only question was how long would it take them to get it working.

Had he known the facts, Holt might have been even more worried. Major Hausmann had rallied his few surviving men and sent them down the railway track to find where the wire break was and repair it. At almost the moment Holt was speculating on the subject as he marched at the head of his band of jubilant ragamuffins, a German soldier was fixing the end of the replaced wire into a spare morse key. He tapped out a signal, got a response from the other end and set to work to tap out the lengthy and urgent message the major had written down for him.

At the rail depot in Adana a bored telegraphist, used to nothing more than the routine messages reporting progress and requisitioning more stores, came alert as the message took shape under his pencil. He was shouting for an orderly before he even had it all down and tapped out an acknowledgement. The orderly went at the double from the telegraph office to the commandant's office.

The commandant read the message with mounting anger. That fool of an engineer officer building the railway had really bungled things! A bridge destroyed, stores destroyed, two trucks destroyed, a train stolen, ten Germans and six native troops killed, all the prisoners escaped! It was incredible. Hausmann would be courtmartialled for this and broken. In the meantime the escapers must be caught and taught a lesson.

The commandant was no fool. The escaping British were not likely to steam into Adana depot in a stolen train. And the track didn't go anywhere else. They would leave the train outside the depot somewhere and head for the port to steal a boat. There was nothing else they could do.

He shouted for Major Guntz and issued his orders rapidly. A squad of troops into the port to guard the boats. Another squad to sweep the land between the railway line and the sea. Shoot on sight – the prisoners have weapons and are dangerous.

Without saying it in words, the commandant managed to imply that he didn't require any prisoners to be brought back.

Guntz clicked his heels and saluted and moved briskly out of the office. And the depot erupted into life as he began barking orders.

It was a fair-sized installation, with the main stores, barracks, a water tower, sidings, carriages and trucks. To the bellowing of noncoms men spilled out of the barrack huts, rifles in hand and piled into the trucks. Four men and a lieutenant climbed on to a railway handcart to go along the track itself.

Major Guntz climbed into the front seat of a staff car alongside the driver. He had two riflemen in the rear seat. He stood up in the car, watching impatiently for the trucks to be ready to follow him and waved his arm forward as a signal to move out.

Because of the clatter of running men, shouted orders and trucks revving their engines, no one had heard the clackety-clack of the approaching train. But as the convoy of trucks started to move out, the train came hurtling down the track at full speed.

The men on the handcart leaped off as the train charged them and ran for safety. Guntz signalled the trucks loaded with soldiers to stop, wondering what was happening. It seemed that the stupid British hoped to drive the train at high speed right through the depot and out the other side.

The onrushing train hit the abandoned handcart on the track at top speed and jumped the rails. It ploughed through the supports of the water tower, sending the tank toppling and pouring out hundreds of gallons of water, sailed on into the main building, demolishing the wall as if it were paper, and crushed the commandant at his desk before it slid to a stop, embedded deep in the building.

For long minutes there was the crash and rumble of falling debris, the scream of steam escaping from the burst boiler of the engine. Then silence.

The engine was still upright, though wrecked. On the crumpled foot plate Raghib lay gathering his last shreds of strength. His right arm was broken and his sleeve was soaked in blood. Neither of his legs would work and from the stabbing pain in his chest he guessed that most of his ribs had gone. He dragged himself to the back of the cab where the box of explosives had been flung by the crash. He slid the box behind himself out of sight and managed to haul himself into a sitting position.

He heard the Germans moving slowly around the wreckage. One of them climbed up into the cab and stared at the blood-spattered figure crouched there. He called down that the driver was still alive and kept Raghib covered with his rifle. Raghib coughed and felt blood welling up into his mouth.

Red-faced with rage at the destruction of the depot, Major Guntz climbed into the cab and pushed the soldier aside. He shouted in German at Raghib, questions and threats. But Raghib was sliding into oblivion and made no effort to understand what the foreigner was saying.

Guntz drew his revolver and pointed it at Raghib's head from two feet away. Raghib's left hand was inside his torn shirt, pressing his aching chest. He could feel his life ebbing away.

'I have something for you,' he mumbled in German.

Major Guntz leaned forward to catch what he was saying. Raghib's hand came slowly out of his shirt holding a grenade with the pin out. Guntz stared at it astounded for a second then he turned and tried to get out of the cab. But the soldier was in the way and there wasn't time.

The grenade exploded, killing Guntz and Raghib and setting off the box of explosives behind him. The wrecked building around the train went up in a tremendous roar, killing most of the soldiers surrounding it.

Holt and his men were well on their way to the sea when they heard the thunder of the explosion behind them and turned to see a dust-cloud climbing into the clear blue sky.

'Raghib's diversion,' said Parks. 'I never thought he'd go through with it. Did you?'

'I never doubted it,' said Holt. 'Keep the men moving.'

'Step lively, lads,' Parks called out. 'Not far to go now and the Germans have got their hands full. They won't be waiting for us at the port.'

In another twenty minutes they had cleared the top of the dunes and were looking down to the shore and the harbour. They could see fishing boats of all sorts and even a small steamer.

'Piece of cake,' said Parks.

'What, Sergeant?'

'Pick the boat you want, sir, and we'll go and get it.'

Holt laughed.

'Step out,' Parks admonished the column. 'You're as good as home.'

Not quite, thought Holt, but we've got a pretty good chance now.

'Shame about Raghib,' said Parks as he marched alongside the lieutenant. 'Still, he turned up trumps for us. I still don't see why he did it.'

'It was his own choice.'

He felt that he understood perfectly well why Raghib had done it and lost his life. Partly it was revenge on the Germans for what they were doing to his country and partly revenge for what they had ordered him to do to the Armenians. And to put an end to his tortured conscience. And perhaps to make some sort of amends to the prisoners he had driven through the desert. A strange mixture of motives. At least he'd gone out with a bang doing something useful.

'If you ask me,' said Parks. 'He couldn't cope with what he'd been through.'

Holt made no comment.

Back in the column Sharp pulled out of his belt the Arab flute that had helped them on the last days of the march to Ras-el-Ain and struck up a tune. The men sang, in good spirits.

'It's a long way to Tipperary,
It's a long way to go . . .'

'Cyprus is where we should head for,' said Parks. 'It can't be more than a few hours straight out to sea. The troopship stopped there when we went out to India. There's a little place I know where we can get a good square meal and a few drinks . . .'

But Holt wasn't even listening.

The column swung along, down towards the harbour, to steal a boat.